IMPACT

By

Donald L. Boone

INTRODUCTION

People often shout at each other while visiting Chatter Box Falls in British Columbia, not in anger, but to be heard over the roar of the wild white water cascading down the one hundred and twenty-five foot waterfall. Where the water from the falls intrudes into the saltwater, a person can, on occasion, look down into the depths and see seven or eight different species of jelly fish pulsating their way through the mixed fresh water and salt brine.

The noise from the cascading water is held in place by the high rock walls of the narrow Fjord. The granite walls of this chamber, nearly a mile high on both sides, has numerous scrub pine trees. These trees, are found scattered throughout the high walls of the canyon on rock ledges where they compete for a foothold of space. Each having struggled to survive here for decades. Their dark green foliage, and dark brown trunks, are but a few of the rare colors that break up the ongoing color of the gray and white granite that surround the eyes in this part of the world.

The huge white waterfall, and its drenching spray, dominate the north end of the Fjord. On the northwest side, just to the east of the waterfall, a small forested area flourishes. These trees, mostly good solid pines, some cedar, maple and madrona, have a ground cover growth of smaller trees and brush.

The Canadian Provincial Government maintains a public park dock at the base of the falls on the west side, with little if any necessities of life available to those who venture the forty-four miles to reach this desolate location. The resident park ranger maintains a small rough cabin for the few months he or she is to be stationed here each year. In addition, there is a hexagonal shaped, open sided communal building with a fire pit in the center, for use by the boating visitors, or members from the youth lodge that is located near the passage through Malibu Rapids into the area. This communal building is located on the original site of the Mac Donald cabin.

In the winter months there are few, if any boaters, who venture into this remote and desolate area. In the winter months, even the park rangers do not inhabit the area. Though it does not happen every year, It is not uncommon for the entire inner basin area to freeze over with an ice sheet of fresh water covering the salt water underneath.

Facing south from the Falls, the southern portion of Princess Louisa Inlet turns to the west where the visitor encounters McDonald Island on the right when leaving, then to pass through Malibu Rapids on the south west side when the tide is favorable. On the north side, on a spit of land at the entrance of the rapids, is the very comfortable lodge for the church youth group. The complex is comprised of several other buildings used for various functions.

Communications with the outside world, from Chatter Box Falls, is impossible by radio at sea level, this because the high forbidding granite walls block the radio transmissions. The canyon walls of Chatter Box Falls are so high, that the summer sun cannot penetrate the area until late morning. Normally to do any communicating with the world, one simply has to leave the area and venture somehow to the outside world.

Everyone interested in venturing to this location knows the only way into Chatter Box Falls is by boat, or float plane. Madeira Park is the nearest town and any source of supplies needed to survive living in the area.

Three couples are en route to this remote spot. Each couple spends nearly every waking moment of their time with their mates. Where you find one of them, you will normally find the other. These three couples are enjoying the summer months exploring the Gulf Island waters of British Columbia, Canada.

Each unaware of the demands about to be put on them just to survive the rigors of mother nature. They are couples who are in tune with each other, and who understand their fellow man. The realities of life are about to be tested with their love and faith in themselves, and the new friends they are about to meet. These three couples will spend the rest of their lives in close unison with each other.

4

SPACE

Both Jake and Victor had been up all night and both were on the edge of irritability from the lack of sleep. The very early morning hours, just before daybreak, seemed to be dragging by. Especially after the long night's work in making some final and critical adjustments on the telescope. Their chosen profession required and demanded this ability of them.

Jake and Victor were actively working on a new prototype telescope for the military. The past several weeks found them making the final adjustments to the telescope for close space work. The telescope had been designed specifically for exploring near space rather than great distances where most large telescopes are normally adjusted to explore.

Even while they were still in school and studying at the university, they were both well aware it could be a hectic life style and both men loved it. Living in close proximity with their colleagues and working long nights in their chosen field of astronomy was what they had both wanted to do since childhood.

To those involved in this field of endeavor it is often very exciting work. These two men were chosen from the multitude of applicants for many reasons. One of the reasons they were chosen came about because of the many personal recommendations they had received, not only from their professors, but from their fellow peers as well. The final item was that they had passed the Intelligence Agency's scrutiny.

Testing the telescope had progressed better than expected recently and they had begun looking for dark objects instead of bright stars or comets in the heavens. Jake kept himself busy using the last hours of their nights work by comparing photographic data from the previous few nights of their work. Even with their assigned tasks in the final adjustments Jake was having problems keeping his mind on the designated military program. He, like most astronomers, was trying to see as far as he could with this telescope into the far reaches of space.

Jake just finished the last comparisons of his computerized photographic data and while he reviewed tonight's data from the telescope, he sat up abruptly, and looking at one of his latest photos, he said, "Vic, come take a look at this."

Victor Danielson was tired, he had a terrible headache and felt like he was suffering from a hangover, though he rarely had much more to drink than an occasional bourbon and water. Reluctantly, he forced himself up out of his chair and walked over to where his partner sat and peered over Jake's shoulder.

"What?" He said. His cranky tone apparent to both of them, and both understood why.

"What do you make of this right here?" Jake said while he pointed to a specific area on the latest computerized photographic printout. His finger rested just under a fair sized point of light. Then he continued, Ithink it looks like a meteor or comet. Although it does seem to be kind of fuzzy."
Victor looked carefully at the photograph. He could easily see what interested Jake, then he said, "No ice trail behind it, so I doubt if it's a comet. Could be a meteor though."

"I don't remember anything being in this section on our last scan of this area. It could have been there, I just don't remember seeing it before."

Their casual conversation continued, "You can check it by looking at the latest data of this area tomorrow. Or before our next scan of this section." Victor wasn't going to encourage any comparison work right now and the film wasn't ready anyway. He was ready to go home to get into bed and get some sleep.

"Hey, maybe I can become famous for discovering a new meteor." Jake said very excitedly.

"Actually, Jake, it'd have to be pretty spectacular to make you famous these days."

Jake reluctantly followed that comment with, "Yeah, I suppose you're right. With the Hubble up there, everyone's finding new things lately."

"I should think so, especially after the asteroid collisions with Jupiter a few years ago."

A week later, after another all night session, Jake was comparing his latest data from the telescope's view of the heavens he now found more interesting. His eyes were tired and he leaned back in the swivel chair, closed his eyes and massaged his eyelids lightly with his fingers. Then he massaged the surrounding area a few moments. Finally a large yawn escaped from him.

Still, as his head tilted to one side he thought, 'Strange.' He looked back at the picture again. It seemed odd for some reason. The object he was comparing from one piece of film to another seemed

7

different somehow. It didn't appear to have moved much when he compared one set of photos against the others. Larger perhaps but still in the same area.

The next day when he woke, which was about two thirty in the afternoon, he decided to get up and eat breakfast. When he'd finished his breakfast of cold cereal with a thinly sliced banana on top, he went to the observatory to check his latest computerized photographs with that of the previous weeks photos.

Mildly surprised, he found the latest picture looked as though the meteor was larger than in the first picture, but fuzzy, or more irregular around the edges than before. 'How could that be?" He thought. 'Larger and fuzzy but hasn't moved."

Three days later, as Jake was lying on his bed in the late afternoon, his eyes closed and with a magazine covering them and his face to cut out the light, he was dozing off in an attempt to get a short nap before the upcoming night's work began. Suddenly he sat straight up. Speaking only to himself he said, "Holy smokes It seems larger only because it's closer to earth now. It's coming straight at us. It's fuzzy because there's more than one meteor, and I'm seeing edges of the others behind the first one. Oh my God, there could be several pieces in a row." He jumped up, struggled into his shoes, not bothering to tie the laces. Grabbing a light jacket he ran to his car feeling the urgent need to get to the observatory and to get some positive confirmation.

ABOARD 'SENSELESS

Larry woke late. He felt slept out and he reached over for Theresa, but she wasn't there. Theresa had gotten up when she heard the child's hand knocking against the hull earlier. She was sitting outside in the aft cockpit of the boat dressed only in her robe enjoying the warmth of the morning sunshine, a nearly empty cup of coffee in her hand, her two cinnamon rolls eaten earlier. Larry climbed out of bed, pulled his shorts on and found a cup in the cupboard and poured himself a cup of coffee. Still carrying the coffee pot in his right hand, he made his way aft to Theresa. "Want a refill Honey?"

"Sure" she said, holding up her cup. Then added, "Your cinnamon rolls are wrapped in foil just behind the loaf of bread."

"Thanks, I'll find 'em." As he moved back inside the boat he recalled how the two boys had rowed out to their boat the evening before taking orders for cinnamon rolls and loaves of bread from them and various other boats anchored around them in Squirrel Cove.

He had been able to over hear the two boys talking to one another as they left Larry and Theresa's boat the evening before. They were discussing the orders they had taken so far. The younger boy holding the list of orders was saying, "We can only take orders for six more loaves of bread and ten more cinnamon rolls."

The older boy at the oars nodded in agreement as he steered toward another boat. It only took two more boats to fill their mom's order list. Then they rowed quickly back to the ramshackle dock in front of their

9

home on the nearby peninsula. Their mother was waiting for their orders when they arrived. When she saw the list, she said, "Thanks, you two." Then as they wandered away she began to prepare her materials for the coming hours of baking.

As was her habit, she would get up about four in the morning to start the baking. This way most everything would still be warm as the small dinghies from the boats would start arriving to pick up their orders. The boys would deliver some of the loaves of bread and cinnamon rolls to some boats as they did on special orders. This was an additional delivery charge, which the boys got to keep for themselves. They never discouraged this, and often offered to make the delivery. It was because of this extra service, that Larry and Theresa had gotten their cinnamon rolls and bread this morning.

Back outside, Larry sat on another deck chair, and he was enjoying his cinnamon rolls when Theresa asked, "When are we going to head home?"

Ithought we'd leave this morning. But I'd like to stop at that big waterfall."

"Which waterfall?" She didn't mind another detour before they went home. She was really enjoying this summer's cruise with Larry on their boat. It was turning out to be the longest period of time they had spent on the boat.

Larry set his coffee cup down on the deck next to his chair, balancing his remaining cinnamon roll on the edge of the chair's arm, and went back into the cabin. He was only gone for a few seconds then he returned with a chart. Unrolling the chart, he pointed to a small area of the chart, and he said, "Right here. It's called Chatter Box Falls and it's supposed to be beautiful."

"Okay, lets go have a look at it."

They sat down to a light breakfast, although they didn't need it after the cinnamon rolls. While they ate their meal, they watched a grandfather on a boat near the shoreline. He was showing his grandson how to feed a nearby eagle. With a flick of the wrist he tossed a bait fish out into the water and away from the stern of the boat.

The eagle was perched in a large, but barren tree just behind them on the dense shoreline, tilting its head from one side to the other. Satisfied, it dropped off the dead tree branch, its large wings spreading silently as it swooped down toward its prey. Just before it reached the water's surface, its legs extended fully, talons at the ready. Quickly, and without effort, its talons dipped easily into the water's surface, the wing tips causing a ripple effect on the water's surface as they moved in unison while it lifted up, and began a long sweeping motion of its wings to regain altitude, the bait fish firmly in its grasp. The eagle's path was now toward a different tree a short distance away where a large nest was apparent. After feeding itself and a chick, it returned to the dead tree branch nearby waiting for the next fish.

Larry could easily enjoy staying here at Squirrel Cove a day or two longer, but he moved to the engine console and turned the keys one at a time, starting the engines on their power boat 'Senseless.' With the engines running smoothly he went out onto his side deck, then walked forward. On the foredeck he pushed the flush deck button, housed inside the water proof cover, with the toe of his shoe.

With the anchor chain rattling, the anchor started coming aboard, and the chain dropped down through the deck, into the chain locker under his feet. It didn't take long to lift the anchor out of the bay's mud bottom as they only had about seventy feet of chain out in this well protected and shallow anchorage.

With the anchor stored away in its deck chocks, Larry and Theresa motored to the west of the small island they had spent so many days near. The anchorage had been quiet but busy, offering the entertainment of watching several boats come and go during their stay here. On one afternoon a float plane had touched down inside the cove. Its large radial engine interrupted the quiet tranquillity of the area. It was delivering a passenger to a sailboat on the west side of the anchorage.

Nearing the entrance leading out of Squirrel Cove, Larry turned the boat to the east and slightly south. Outside he turned southerly and pushed the throttles forward slowly. When the boat came up to speed, he eased the throttles back slightly letting the boat settle into a comfortable cruising speed.

ABOARD 'TIME OUT

Ken and Helen had just cast their dinghy mooring lines loose from the government docks in Nanaimo British Columbia. They had finished shopping at the nearby supermarket and stored their groceries haphazardly in the bow of the small boat. Like many others they had used a shopping cart belonging to the large mall across the street from the marina to get their groceries down to the floating dock. It only took Ken a few moments to return the shopping cart back to the parking lot, and a cart storage area.

With their outboard motor pushing the small boat, they moved slowly out from between the two floating docks, finally to turn left at the end of the dock. Seconds later they were turning right around the large stone corner of the seawall. The perimeter around the boating basin had been constructed out of large quarried stones. As they motored slowly past the fuel dock on their left, Ken began to look across the open waterway toward the anchorage on the east side of Newcastle Island, already in visual search of their boat anchored there.

As they passed the end of the long new pier now offering more protection to the marina basin area, a float plane took off from the commercial air flight dock just behind them. The roar of its large radial engine faded into the distance as they made the crossing from Nanaimo to the anchorage at Newcastle Island. A few minutes later Ken nudged the bow of the rubber boat into the side of their sailboat 'Time Out' When Helen was aboard he handed her all their groceries, then he tied the small boat to the stern of the larger boat and he climbed up the stern boarding ladder.

Helen put the groceries away while Ken put the blocks of ice into the bottom of their icebox. When he'd finished he went up the four steps and into the cockpit of the boat. Just about ready to make the crossing of Georgia Straight, he looked once again at the smoke stacks to the south of the city. The smoke still appeared to be going straight up. This was common knowledge to boaters that the smoke from the mill would give an indication of the wind conditions out on the straight. The indication Ken was seeing was that there was little, if any, wind outside the protection of the island where they were anchored, and that they would most likely have to motor across unless some afternoon breezes filled in.

Helen, also ready, stood by the helm until Ken had the anchor pulled up and stored in the bow locker. Finally, ready to go, she put the engine transmission in gear and motored out of the basin and the myriad of other boats in the anchorage. She headed their boat north around the northern end of Newcastle Island, then east toward their destination of this day, Pender Harbour.

The trip across Georgia Straight went well. It seemed to be a shorter trip than normal, partly due to the quiet water on the crossing. They dropped their anchor in the Garden Bay area of Pender Harbour that afternoon, with the intention of topping up their fuel tank the following morning. Then they would head inland to the waterfall they had heard so much about.

The next afternoon, and well into their trip, they became aware of a fairly large power boat coming up off their stern as both boats traveled through one of the long fjords. As the powerboat drew closer, the owner of the boat slowed his vessel so as not to cause a large wake when he passed the sailboat. After passing by them slowly, he cut across Ken's bow making it easier for Ken to cut through what little wake he had left behind him. Ken noted the name on the stern. 'Senseless.'

'A considerate boater.' Ken thought. 'I'll thank him if I see him later down the line.'

Later in the afternoon as Ken and Helen came along-side the Provincial Government docks at Chatter Box Falls, forty miles inland from Pender Harbour, Ken saw the power boat that had passed them earlier in the day. He would make a point of going by the boat and invite the owners down for a visit and perhaps something to sip on during their time aboard.

NEIGHBORS

Frank had seen the boat on the inside of the dock, leave in the early morning hours and he wanted to move in there to get off the incoming traffic side. He wouldn't worry as much, about being bumped into by another boat, if he was on the inside. He hadn't been bumped by other boats before, it was just part of his nature to worry. Picking up his coffee cup, he walked up the dock. Arriving at the empty spot he measured it by eye and he felt he and Jessie could get their boat into this spot. A man on the boat to his right stepped out onto the dock and moved to his side, as if to help him ascertain if he could get into the only open space on this side. He said to Frank, "Think you'll fit?"

"Should. Might be close though?"

The man standing next to him stuck out his hand and said, "I'm Charles."

"Frank," he said extending his own hand.

"I can help guide you in Frank. I might even be able to pull my boat back a bit to give you more room if you need it."

"Thanks. I think it's big enough for me to get into. But I will accept the guiding hand if you don't mind."

"Not at all. Are you ready now?"

"Sure am, I'll only be a few minutes." Frank turned and walked back to his boat.

"Jessie, we're gonna move up to that empty spot on the inside," he said as he started the boat's engine.

"Okay, Honey." She started going through a routine that was second nature now.

Jessie cast their dock lines loose, and moved the fenders to the other side as Frank motored them away from the spot where they had been moored for the last few days. They made their way around the southern end of the dock into the backwater behind it. When they got to the empty spot, Frank put the engine's transmission into reverse and backed the boat speed down briefly, allowing it to drift into the dock. Charles Jensen took Jessie's bow line from her, and cleated it off temporarily. By now Frank was on the dock tying up the stern line.

Finished, Frank invited Charles aboard for coffee, and he'd accepted his new neighbor's invitation. A few minutes later, Charles wife, Mary, found them and joined them.

VISITORS

Loyd and Lyn had made their way inland in their sailboat, 'Itchy Feet', from Madeira Park in Pender Harbour. The weather had been comfortably warm, but it also lacked enough wind to sail. Most of the distance they traveled was spent between high rock walls on either side. Several small waterfalls dotted the landscape along the way, each spilling into the salt water at the base of the rocks. Any trace of wind being blocked as they traveled, they motored the entire distance through the long fjords.

At one point during the passage inland through the desolate area, Loyd rigged up the air pressurized shower water tank, while Lyn heated water on their propane stove. She mixed hot water from the stove with cold water from the tanks, this providing nice warm water for their shower. She retrieved towels and wash cloths from the small bathroom, and when all was ready, the two of them took showers in the cockpit.

They were able to do this in leisure while the boat's electric autopilot kept the boat on its course straight down the center of the fjord. They washed themselves, then began toweling dry in the warmth of the afternoon sun. It left them feeling quite refreshed. Rather than getting dressed, they stayed nude enjoying the warmth of the day on their bodies, dressing only as they neared the south end of Queen's Reach. From this point they were aware it would only be a short time before they were back in the company of other people.

It was early fall, the part of the season where the trees just begin to turn different hues. Various shades of yellow were becoming evident. Along the banks, and high rocky areas, chipmunks could be seen scurrying to and from their dens in a final rush to fill their larders.

A few days after arriving at Chatter Box Falls, one morning, when Loyd got up, he felt a chill in the morning air. He decided to light a fire in their small heating stove located in the main salon of the boat. Lyn lay snuggled under the covers in the Vee berth knowing Loyd would return shortly. She would get him warm again while they waited for the stove to perform its magic warming the main cabin. Lyn's mind reflected how most days like this are, as a rule, pretty hum drum. Nothing out of the ordinary would normally be taking place. But today they had been invited to have lunch with Ken and Helen Dougherty on their sailboat 'Time Out' and Lyn had agreed to bring homemade cinnamon rolls.

"Want to fool around Babe?" Loyd said, as he quickly crawled back into the warmth of their bed.

"Sounds good to me, but I've got to get up and mix the dough for the cinnamon rolls so it will have time to rise before baking. How about after lunch instead?" She marveled, as she thought about all their years together. They still had a very active sex life.

Loyd said with a grin, "Okay. Works for me."

They lay snuggling for a few more minutes. She pressed her breasts against him and she could feel him rising against her skin. She also knew that if she didn't get up now she would change her mind.

19

She raised up, and crawled over him to get out of the Vee berth. As she did so, she let her breasts brush his face teasing him.

About a quarter to twelve, there came a knock on their coach roof. Loyd got up from where he had been reading, set the book down on the starboard settee, walked the few steps aft, and pulled the main hatch open over his head. The sweet smell of cinnamon rolls escaped into the air around him as he poked his head out the main hatch to see Ken standing there. Ken, a tall slender man, with dark hair, always seemed to be clean shaven. Ken was standing on the sun bleached floating Ferro-cement dock.

"Loyd, you two about ready?"

"Yeah, Lyn's just waiting for the cinnamon rolls to cool a bit more so she can put some icing on them."

"Okay, I'm on my way down to the power boat, 'Senseless', to tell Larry and Theresa that we're about ready for lunch. I'll see you two at our boat in a few minutes then."

"Larry and Theresa?" Loyd said questioningly.

"Oh. I guess you haven't met them yet"

Idon't think so"

From below Ken heard Lyn call out, "Ken, we'll be ready shortly."

"Okay, Lyn." Ken smiled as he turned and started walking up the dock toward the falls. Saying, "See ya," as he left.

A short time later, as Loyd and Lyn were walking down the dock, two small boys who were squatted on the edge of the dock trying to net some small fish, spotted the baking pan in Lyn's hand. They stood as Loyd and Lyn were passing by and quickly offered to eat some of her cinnamon rolls.

Lyn paused and smiled. A naturally generous person, she handed the pan to Loyd. While he held it she pulled one of the larger rolls loose from the others in the pan, and tore it in half. "You probably won't like these." She said as she handed half to each of the boys.

"Softy, and you know as well as I do those two boys will remember who you are," Loyd said to her as he handed the pan back to her. But, he knew she was always that way, especially toward children. He also knew that if they were here very long, every child around would know about Lyn's cinnamon rolls, maybe most of the adults as well.

When they got closer to the stern of the sailboat, 'Time Out', they could see another couple already on board with Ken and Helen.

Ken stood and offered a hand to Lyn as she said, "Permission to board captain?" using the standard courtesy among boaters.

"Absolutely. Anyone toting fresh cinnamon rolls doesn't need permission to come aboard this boat," Ken said with a touch of humor in his voice.

Loyd followed close behind Lyn as she boarded, then out of habit patted her on the butt as he stepped down into the cockpit with her. When he looked up, he caught sight of a grin on the face of the new lady he had not met as yet. He knew she had seen his hand move affectionately to Lyn's back side.

Ken introduced them saying, "Lyn, Loyd, this is Larry and Theresa from the power boat, Senseless."

"Lyn, I'm glad to meet anyone who makes fresh home made cinnamon rolls," Larry said. Then he stuck out his hand to Loyd. "They must call you lucky Loyd, to have a lady who knows how to bake this kind of stuff."

Loyd knew which boat this couple was from. He had passed it while he walked down the dock toward the beach earlier in the day. He stuck his hand out welcoming the introduction to the new couple. "Hi Larry. . It's kind of strange to find a power boater among sail boaters. Of course with a boat name like yours, I guess you're aware you chose the wrong type of vessel."

"Well, I've found that all you rag sailors aren't really a bad lot," he chuckled. They were all aware of the ongoing, mostly friendly war between the two types of boaters. Sail boaters' insisted on the right of way to keep the wind in their sails, and most often power boaters gave way.

After the lunch of various cheeses, salami, fresh crab, three different kinds of small crackers and wine, they had started to indulge themselves in the freshly baked cinnamon rolls.

"Lyn, I'd love to know how you do this," Theresa said, after licking the caramelized sugar remains from her finger tips. "My mom wasn't really a homebody, so I never learned to do this sort of thing when I lived at home."

"If you're free tomorrow afternoon, why don't you come down to our boat, 'Itchy Feet', and I'll show you how it's done. It's really quite easy to do."

"I'd love to. Any particular time?"

"When you get there works for me."

"Thanks Lyn, anything I should bring?"

"No. I have everything we'll need, besides then Loyd and I will get to share in the finished product, as if we need it," she said. At the same time she reached out and patted Loyd's small, but rounding tummy.

The six of them continued to talk about various topics, where they were from, what they did for a living and where they had planned to go after leaving Chatter Box Falls. Ken and Larry were telling Loyd about some good anchorages up in the Desolation Sound area that he and Lyn hadn't been to as yet. The women talked about storage of needed goods on their various boats and living aboard.

Theresa, a slender blond and bubbly individual, also seemingly a very naive person, explained how she rarely worried about long term storage because they never stayed out anywhere very long. "This is the first really long vacation we've spent on the boat."

Helen and Lyn, both apparently having spent more time cruising, answered several questions as Theresa asked them about how they managed their long term food storage and laundry. Also, how they kept in touch with their families and other assorted questions that most boaters never become aware of until they become interested in long term cruising, whether the cruising trips were long or short distances. The six of them spent the entire afternoon together, the friendship blossoming.

The day had slipped by quickly, and the evening sky was beginning to show signs of losing the light. The high granite canyon walls blocked the late afternoon sun's rays penetrating the fjord, so it grew dark early and quickly in the depths of the park near the waterfall.

A few folks who had been enjoying the last rays of penetrating sunlight, suddenly becoming aware that the evening sky was getting brighter again, instead of darker as it should be.

"Hey, what's with the sky?" someone said, and several people began to look up. It continued to get brighter until it was so bright that anyone looking up had to shield their eyes against the bright sky. The brightness lasted a few seconds, when suddenly everyone in the area was hammered by an explosive sonic boom.

The intensity was of such magnitude that it knocked some people off their feet. Some small children were crying and holding their hands over their ears. Little did this group of people know, but they had been spared most of the sonic shock wave because of the high canyon walls surrounding, and protecting them.

THE DAY THE EARTH SHOOK

Sometime after the noise and bright light stopped, the earth began to shake savagely. Rocks, large and small, began to rain down from the high walls of the canyon splashing into the water all around the area and leaving small waves racing from shoreline to shoreline and back again. Trees of all sizes toppled from the perches they had previously held on to so tenaciously for many years, their roots often still hanging onto the rocks that had held them in place. Birds of all kinds took flight, and with no apparent place to land safely, they all were screeching loudly in protest.

It seemed to everyone as though they were having the largest earthquake in history. The shaking seemed to last forever and it took several minutes for the major upheavals to subside. When it was over, most folks were either laying down on some kind of a flat surface, or down on their hands and knees. Some were holding onto any thing they could use for support. Fear showing in the eyes of most, children were crying as well as some adults, and most were praying. Some boats had broken loose from their moorings at the dock and the owners were scrambling to get them tied to the dock again.

Larry and Loyd were helping others secure their boats as the two of them worked their way up the dock toward their own boats to check for damage. As the two of them moved up the dock, they looked around as they went. They became aware of the park ranger in the distance trying to secure one of the steel dock cables onto a tree on the shoreline. They looked at each other, nodded in agreement, and without saying a word went to help the park ranger secure the cable.

Brian, a young man of slender build, still suffering from acne, saw them coming to help and hollered at them. "Hurry, please hurry." Loyd turned around and hollered back at Lyn to check their boat. He saw her nod her head yes in agreement. When they arrived where Brian was struggling, he gave instructions to each of them as they secured the dock to the tree with cable and some cable clamps he had found in a spare parts box in his cabin.

The havoc of the falling rocks and trees had stopped, but the birds were still nervous, many were still screeching loudly while in flight. Brian said to the two of them, have an antenna placed high up on the hill. Later I'll see if I can call out on the radio and find out what the hell happened"

When they had finished securing the dock to the tree, Loyd and Larry headed back toward their own boats. When they got to Larry's boat everything seemed to be okay.

Then, on Loyd's boat, they found Lyn and Theresa on board. Lyn greeted them with, "Everything seems to be fine here." By now most of the water that had been thrashing back and forth in the basin, had quieted leaving only the normal ripples on the surface.

Very few slept well that night but they knew they couldn't leave in the dark of night. Some stayed up all night, or took turns sleeping, trying to be ready for anything. One group had spent hours during the dark of night on the dock talking with each other, just getting to know one their boating neighbors. A propane powered lantern in the center of the group offered a quieting, even a warming effect.

Early the following morning Brian, the park ranger, came down the dock to 'Itchy Feet' and found Larry, Loyd and Ken having tea in the cockpit.

"Come aboard, Brian," Loyd said, indicating with a wave of his hand to an empty place near him. Brian climbed over the raised cockpit combing, and the winch fastened there. His uniform, was a little rumpled and dirty. It was apparent that he had probably slept in it. As he sat Lyn reached out from the small galley inside the boat, handing him a cup of tea.

"Would you like milk or sugar in that?"

"Thank you, no," then he continued, "Well gentlemen, my radio antenna is badly mangled on the ground up there." He indicated the rocky slopes above them. Ican't get to it because of a rock slide"

"I guess the only way to get news of what happened would be to go out to Pender Harbour then?" Larry said. All of them were aware of the inability to transmit on a radio down here at sea level on the docks because of the high rocky walls surrounding them.

"That's about it. The problem is, I don't have enough fuel in my small boat to make the trip out and my relief isn't due for another two weeks, so we'll need to find a volunteer to go out and get the news."

"Why don't we just wait for another boat to come in and get the news from them?" asked Ken.
"Sounds logical to me," Loyd said. "There should be someone arriving in the next day or so."

"You're probably right," Brian agreed, and so it was left at that, even though they were all concerned.

But no boats came, and no boats left.

BOMBARDMENT

The meteorite came into the earth's atmosphere at such a shallow angle that it could have easily skipped like a flat rock on a pond of water. The first one didn't, however. Instead it dug a long ever deepening trench into the south Texas earth. It came to rest just south, and west of Lions Texas.

Shortly after the meteorite collided with the earth's surface causing the primary crater, several fragmented pieces of this same meteorite joined with the earth's surface, one after the other. In their process of colliding with the earth, each fragment dug a long trough. The troughs starting out small, but progressed in width and depth as they came to rest in the Texas soil. In all they created a series of long deep ditches reaching to the edge of the Gulf Coast.

Another meteorite fragment, impacted the earth's surface just off the south east coast of Nova Scotia. The wave it caused was sent in a southerly direction, and some wave damage was done to the communities at Glace Bay, around the southern end of the coast.

Yet little life was lost due to the lack of large communities along this area. One ferry en-route to St. Johns, Nova Scotia had capsized, and all lives were lost. There was no time to send an SOS signal for help. Still, no one could have come to their rescue.

Early the next day another meteorite fragment came down in Russia. In the following days, two more came down in China, one in the Philippine Sea, one small fragment impacted the Arctic polar ice cap. In almost every case, huge amounts of land mass was disturbed.

Tectonic plates were forced to give way, the earth's surface welling up in waves like slow wiggling Jello.

KILLING WAVE

The huge wave started at the edge of the now scarred Texas coastline, careened off the north east coast of the Yucatan peninsula like ripples in a pool after a rock had been dropped into its shallow depth. Only this large ripple, a thirty foot wave, was wiping the land's end clean of vegetation, and any living life in its direct path.

About the same time, an extension of this wave also collided with the northwest coast of Cuba. It killed 2703 people before it was finished washing over the end of the island. It was due to reach the Cayman Islands shortly thereafter, where life could cease to exist.

Jamaica was the next in line to feel the wrath of a watery death. On the other side of Cuba, the wave was beginning to collide with, and sweeping over the Bahama Island group. Another similar wave was heading south from the North Atlantic. A heavy earthquake off the coast of Petropavlovsk Kamchatskiy, Russia started a high Tsunami wave. It was reaching out in all directions with a vast Pacific Ocean to travel across. Japan was the first to feel its tentacles

TURBULENT WATERS

Late in the morning the water in Princess Louisa Inlet started dropping, it caught everyone off guard. The water level kept going down until three boats, that had been anchored between the waterfall and the high granite wall to the west, were aground.

The park dock was slowly working its way down the retaining pilings, the dock's galvanized pipe retaining straps were cutting shellfish off the pilings with loud crunching noises from where they had been growing just under the water line. Broken shells floating lazily downward toward the bottom of the bay.

Just before the boats at the north end of the dock were about to touch the bottom, the water slowed its decent, until finally it stopped receding. Then, after a time it started to slowly rise again. Earlier, Loyd and Larry, had gone down to the main Malibu Lodge to see if anyone was aware of what was going on. What they found was everyone outside watching the water at the mouth of Malibu Rapids going down to such a level that a boat of any size could not pass through the waterway entrance. Standing on the deck of the lodge with everyone else they watched in awe.

Suddenly someone shouted, "Look, look down there." In the distance everyone could see a large saltwater swell moving up the waterway, not a breaking wave, just a large body of slowly moving ocean saltwater. The water had receded similarly to the prior events of a Tsunami wave, and now it was returning.

As the water got to the corner of Queen's Reach, it flowed slowly up around the corner, over the top of a small breakwater, then easily washed out a low lying cabin, on skids, that was left over from one of the many logging operations in the area.

"Larry, come on we've got to get back and warn the folks at the falls," said Loyd in a rush as he started turning to run. The two of them raced down to the rubber dinghy and jumped aboard. The outboard engine purred to life on the first pull and they raced away. Just as they were rounding the corner past Mc Donald Island and were heading toward the dock, Larry said, "I see the beginning of the wave crest passing the entrance and the lodge. It looks like it will breach the entrance rocks."

Ahead of them they shouted for everyone on the docks to beware of the incoming water. Of course no one understood. When they were on the dock, they took more time to explain what was coming. The water in the park basin started to rise slowly, but steadily. Most of its brute strength had already been spent just reaching this desolate area. Brian, the park ranger, who was at the time, on the dock got the men together and they prepared to keep the dock in place using boat engines if need be. The dock retaining straps were just a few inches from the top of the shortest pilings when the rising water finally stopped. A sigh of relief was heard as someone reported that the water seemed to be dropping slightly.

Later that day when the water level had settled, the earth began to shake again. It was thought, by most, to be another heavy earthquake as there was no sonic boom to accompany it this time. Brian had gone down to the lodge and found that the high water had reached the foundation of the lodge and filled the empty swimming pool before it had subsided. Even after the large wave had passed, the water level still seemed higher than it had been before, though the pool had begun to drain. In reality the earth in the area had dropped to a noticeable lower level.

Brian found the people at the lodge voicing their desire to get out of the area so they could go home to their families. Most had come in by float planes or a ferry that occasionally serviced the lodge. No one was in a panic as yet, but several were close to it.

THE DECISION

Loyd, Larry and Ken had become friendly in this short time. Not close friends yet, but friends who became confident that the other person would be there to help when the need arose. The three of them were standing at the ramp leading from the floating park dock to the land nearby, having a discussion with the park ranger Brian.

Brian was concerned about having the ability to get out to Pender Harbour to see what had happened and was saying, "I'm supposed to stay here and look after the park. I mean, this place is my responsibility. But I'm worried about my wife and kids."

Ken nodded his head in agreement and commented, "Brian, I'm sure your superintendent would understand your feelings, and the park isn't going any place is it?"

Brian picked up the conversation again. "Then there's the matter of the people at the lodge. They're wanting to get out of here in the worst way."

Loyd, thinking it over, said, "Well, Brian, I'm willing to take some folks out, but I can't take many at a time on my boat."

"Me too," Ken added.

"Actually my boat's the better one to make a trip like this," Larry said. "It's bigger, faster, and I think I could take everyone out in one trip." Larry's boat, although an older boat, was forty two feet in length and had a twelve foot beam. These factors did make it ideal, and its twin Grey Marine engines would provide plenty of horsepower.

The men stood there for a moment in silence. Then acting as if the decision had been made, Brian said, "Larry, I want to go out with you when you go. I've got to get to my family." He hadn't meant to say it this way, but the four of them knew Brian didn't care what happened to the park, he wanted to get home, and he wanted to go now.

"Have you got enough fuel Larry?" Loyd asked, as if allowing Larry an out if he wanted to take it.

Larry didn't mind making the trip, but he would have liked to have been the one to say so. "Yes. Plenty. Well, at least I have enough to get out to Pender Harbour, and I can fuel up before I come back."

"When can we leave?" Brian asked.

"As soon as you like, I suppose?"

Once it had been agreed to go, Ken said, "I'll go along with Larry as a deck hand. Loyd, will you look after my lady and my boat?"

"You betcha, Ken."

Then Larry thought about the possibility of some danger and said, "Ken, can Theresa stay with Helen while we're gone?"

"I'm sure Helen would welcome her."

Plans were made for Larry and Ken to leave the following morning when slack tide would allow them to pass through Malibu Rapids safely. Though the rocky opening through Malibu Rapids appeared larger it was because the rocky landscape had sunk deeper beneath the waters surface. Not being certain of the new depth, they did not want to take any chances. Helen and Theresa both offered resistance to the idea of them going, but gave in when Larry and Ken reasoned with them, convincing them that they would be okay.

CALAMITY

Six thirty in the morning the alarm clock went off waking Larry. Groggy, he forced himself out of bed. He and Theresa had gotten used to sleeping late in the mornings while on the boat. With the rigors of home and the city life forgotten, they would sleep until they woke up naturally. Even then, they would squander time away lying around for a period of time before getting up.

After he got dressed he put the teakettle on the propane stove, turned the knob to the light position and when the gas started to flow in the burner, he touched the match to it. The low "whump" was a prelude to the water for their coffee getting hot.

Larry, satisfied the propane burner was working okay, walked over to the main engine console, and flipped on the switch marked, 'Blowers'. He let the blowers run, venting any gas fumes out of the engine compartment for a few minutes before he turned the key on number one engine. The engine started immediately and he let it run a couple of minutes before he started number two engine, then he turned the blowers off.

As the engines warmed up, he pulled two coffee cups out of the cupboard, found the instant coffee, and when the water was hot, he made two cups of coffee. He put some sugar into his own cup, dropped the spoon into the sink and started forward with the hot coffee.

In the forward stateroom he set the cups down on top of a built in locker, and reached over to gently shake Theresa's shoulder. "Sweetheart, time to wake up."

"Umm," she mumbled reluctantly, turning over, away from him. She'd been awake, and she'd heard the engines start, she was just enjoying the warmth and comfort of their bed.

"Come on Sweetie, time to get moving."

"I need some coffee first," she said, stalling.

He knew her morning game well by now. "Got it right here."

Theresa sat up leaned back against the built in head board, her light blue night gown clinging to her sensually as she accepted her coffee.

"Gotta go check on the engine temperatures Sweetie. See you when you get up." He would rather have climbed back into bed with her. She looked very inviting.

Theresa had a feeling about the trip Larry was going to make today. It wasn't a good feeling, but she knew he would make it no matter what she said, or did, because he had committed himself. She finished her coffee, got out of bed, and dressed in silence. Then she went aft to the main cabin where Larry was watching the engine temperature and oil pressure gauges as the engines warmed up.

"Larry, will you please be careful today. I'm worried that something might go wrong."

"No problem Babe. With everything that's happened in the last few days, Ken and I will be very wary."

They made small talk as they each ate a bowl of cold cereal.

"You have enough fuel to make it round trip?"

"Possibly, but I'll top our tanks up before I come back anyway."

"You need more money?"

"No, I've got enough."

Theresa knew she couldn't stall him any longer. When they had finished eating Theresa rinsed their dishes and left them in the stainless steel sink to finish later. She gathered up a warm jacket and her purse, then the two of them climbed off the boat and walked down the dock to the sailboat 'Time Out' where Ken and Helen were waiting for their arrival.

"Permission to board skipper?" Larry called out after he had knocked on the coach roof .

Ken popped his head up out of the companion way hatch and said, "Welcome aboard Larry, Theresa. Come on in out of the chill."

Inside, while they were talking about the trip out to Pender Harbour, Ken reached into his hanging locker and got his wind breaker. Then he went aft and pulled a life jacket out from behind a box of stored food.

"How long do you think it will take us to get to Pender Harbour, Larry?"

"It shouldn't take us long to get there. Maybe four hours or so."

"That long in a powerboat, huh?" He knew, it could take almost twice that long in a sailboat under power at an easy cruising speed.

"If it was just the two of us, it wouldn't take that long. But, with a boat load of people it will be slower going. Plus the time we spend getting them loaded aboard at the lodge."

"Yeah, that could be fun in itself," Ken remarked.

Ken kissed Helen before he started out of the boat. Then as the guys were leaving, Helen and Theresa waved goodbye to them, telling them to be careful. They waved back and assured them they would be. When they boarded Larry's boat, 'Senseless', the steam from the engine exhaust pipes wafted up in the morning air leaving a slight fuel odor. Larry said "Ken, if you will take the bow line when we cast off this dock, and again when we get to the lodge dock, I'll take care of the stern line."

"Works for me," Ken said.

"Okay, let's do it."

Ken walked up the dock, still damp from the morning dew, and untied the bow line on the forward dock cleat. He then held the line in one hand as he walked aft. He left the fenders hanging over the side of the boat in readiness for their arrival at the lodge dock.

When he was amidships, he held onto the life line stanchions while Larry untied the stern line. Then Larry climbed aboard.

Once Larry was back at the engine controls he called out to Ken, "Okay partner, push off and climb aboard." Ken shoved the hull hard, having to dig his heels in to get the boat moving out away from the dock. Once it started to move, he stepped up onto the boat's side deck. On board he laid the bow line down on the side deck and wrapped it around a mid ship cleat to keep it in place. After Ken had moved inside the boat's cabin, he stood by Larry watching as Larry very skillfully maneuvered the boat further away from the dock by using his engines to turn the boat, almost within its own length.

Several minutes later they pulled up to the dock at the lodge, and Ken had moved out to the side deck as Larry nudged 'Senseless' up to the dock. Ken easily stepped down onto the dock, and casually walked forward to secure the bow line to a dock cleat. Larry was tying up the stern by the time he was through with his bow line and had turned around to face aft. They left the engines idling as they walked up to the lodge to see if their eager passengers were ready.

ABANDONING

Todd and Beverly had been tossing and turning for two hours, finally they had given up trying to get any sleep. It was after two o'clock in the morning when they got up and started making their final preparations to leave. Loading their small motor home with the remaining personal items they wanted to take took the remainder of the night. Beverly spent hours the day before at the market in Madeira Park buying food, canned juices, bottled water and soda pop.

The store, jammed to capacity with people, had little room left for any kind of normal shopping. People's carts were full to overflowing. They were buying up as much as they could pack out and get home. Luckily, the stores in the area had been maintaining their high food stocks for the summer visitors that always invaded the area. Beverly had found places to store stuff in their motor home she hadn't even known existed before.

Just after seven thirty she told Todd, "Honey, I have every thing stuffed in there that I can get in."

Todd was just closing the hood after checking the water and oil. The battery water was up, as was the brake fluid and power steering fluid. "Might as well get started, eh?"

"Okay. I'll lock up the house. Are you sure you wan'na leave the jeep?"

"No sense locking the house, Luv. If somebody wants in they'll just break in anyway. There's no sense taking two vehicles. It'd just cost us twice as much to travel, and I rather we were traveling together in the same vehicle."

Beverly reluctantly closed the back door of their home, climbed up into the cab of the motor home where Todd had already seated himself. She looked around once more at the home they had lived in for twelve years. A tear slowly found its way down her cheek as Todd started the engine, and backed out of the driveway. He didn't want to leave either, but he felt it was necessary.

Beverly hated to leave this small town. She knew all their neighbors. They had spent many hours visiting one another, having pot luck dinners or playing cards together one or two times a month. It had been the most comfortable place she had ever lived. Now, they were committing themselves to the trip, heading for Tennessee, and her original family hometown.

THE LOADING

When Larry and Ken pushed the lodge door open and walked into the lobby, they found Brian McCormick waiting for them. Standing beside him was another man they did not know. When the four of them came together, Brian introduced them to Mr. Foley, explaining that he was the lodge manager.

When the introductions were done, Larry said, "we're ready when you folks are, Mr. Foley."

"Thank you. I'll get everyone together and we'll come down to the dock right away."

Larry nodded his approval and he and Ken turned and walked out of the lodge retracing their route back down to the waiting powerboat. It was only a few minutes before they saw several people starting down the ramp to the dock toward them.

Larry climbed aboard the boat so he would be in position to instruct everyone where he wanted them to sit or stand. He needed to balance the trim of the boat with their weight. A few seconds after the group arrived on the dock, Ken popped his head into the cabin and said, "Larry, there are twenty-eight people out here, all loaded down with baggage."

"Holy cow! Twenty eight people?" he said in disbelief. It hadn't even entered his mind to ask how many people he would be taking. Idon't know if we can get that many in here."

Larry went out to the dock where he found Brian and Mr. Foley. "Brian, twenty eight people is a bit much."

Mr. Foley said, "These people are really desperate to get out of here. Can we put some of them on deck? I'm sure they would be willing."

"Possibly. But I'll tell you right off, we won't be able to take them and their luggage. They'll have to leave the luggage here and come back for it later."

"Ummm. . . okay. Just a minute.. Let me explain the problem to them."

Mr. Foley approached the group and they clustered around him as he began to explain the situation to them. He only spent a few minutes, then he returned. "They all agree and understand the situation." In the distance, behind Mr. Foley, several men were hauling luggage back inside the lodge.

Several of the women had opened their luggage and removed some changes in underwear and other personal items that they put into their purses. Larry was sure some of the purses must weigh as much as some luggage they were leaving behind, but he knew better than to get between these women and their purses. What was in those purses would stay in them.

Larry thought about the circumstances of having this many people on board, then said, "Okay, and if we need to have anyone on deck, you arrange for those who are on deck to be rotated below deck, say, every ten or fifteen minutes, so that we don't have anyone falling overboard from the cold wind chill factor." He knew life jackets were out of the question.

"I'll do that," Mr. Foley said gratefully. Larry had the feeling that Mr. Foley rather liked being in charge of this group.

When they were all on board the boat, Larry switched several people around to level the boat in the water. The group filled the whole main cabin area below deck, what Vee berth area that could be occupied, and the aft cockpit area as well. The only people huddled on the foredeck were those smoking and there was barely room for them below when they wished to come down and join the rest of the group. Larry insisted that no one could smoke below deck, or in the cabin area of the boat. With everyone settled down, the boat was now floating five and a half inches deeper in the water. Unhappy with the situation, Larry motioned for Ken to cast their lines loose from the dock and to get aboard.

Larry backed the boat slowly out away from the dock, put the transmission in forward gear, and moved carefully out and through the quiet waters of Malibu Rapids. Once outside in Queen's Reach they turned to the south and started the long slow journey to Pender Harbour. Ken worked his way into the interior of the boat next to Larry at the helm and engine throttles, then said, Ithink we're lucky this is a quiet water time of the day."

"You got that right. If it was rough, we couldn't make this trip with this many people on board. She's kind of sluggish as it is."

Larry silently pointed to the knotmeter and Ken saw they were only making five knots. "Let's hope it stays this way for the next few hours."

The first four hours were on very smooth water and they had been able to make better time than expected. About midway through the fifth hour they began to meet ocean swells that wouldn't normally be found in Prince of Wales Reach.

By the end of the sixth hour, and at a reduced speed, it was becoming a problem with salt water spraying up over the deck soaking anyone that might have ventured up there. The cockpit curtains around the aft portion of the boat were successful in keeping those people in that part of the boat dry and offered them some degree of warmth as well.

When they neared the west end of Agamemnon Channel and Nelson Island, Larry quietly said to no one in particular, "My God, what's wrong with this picture." Ken, standing nearby said, "What's wrong?"

"You've navigated these waters. Look out forward of our port bow and tell me if I'm dreaming."

Ken studied the view ahead of them for a few seconds, not believing what he saw. Ahead, where there should be an abundance of land and many islands, they saw only a few semi-large, and very few small islands, some with low lying connecting land bridges. Mostly, they were viewing what seemed to be almost open ocean. Apparently most of the south end of Texada Island and Lasqueti Island had vanished. In the distance a faint view of what could be part of the Washington Cascade Mountain range appeared through the haze.

"This is impossible," Ken said to Larry.

Larry turned on the FM radio and turned the tuner until he found a station that was broadcasting. There was a broken news report being broadcast. In between bursts of static, Larry, Ken and those close enough to hear the news were greeted with a news report that said,

IT IS NOW BEING CONFIRMED THAT A LARGE METEORITE LANDED IN SOUTH WEST TEXAS, IN THE UNITED STATES. APPARENTLY IT WAS SEVERAL MILES FROM THE COAST, BUT THE DAMAGE WAS EXTENSIVE. SEA WATER IS NOW SOAKING UP SOME OF THE PRIME FARM LANDS QUITE A DISTANCE INLAND. IT HAS ALSO BEEN CONFIRMED THAT A NUMBER OF OTHER METEORITES HAVE IMPACTED EARTH AS WELL. THESE LOCATIONS AND THE DAMAGE DONE ARE NOT KNOWN, BY THIS STATION AT THIS TIME. THE RESULTS OF THE METEORITE IMPACTS HAVE APPARENTLY CAUSED SEVERAL CONTINENTAL PLATES TO SHIFT SUDDENLY AND SOME ARE STILL SHIFTING. THE RESULTS, AS WE UNDERSTAND IT, INVOLVE A DEVASTATING LOSS OF LIFE AND LAND. PLATES ARE STILL SHIFTING, NOT ONLY IN THE UNITED STATES, BUT SEVERAL OTHER PLACES WORLD WIDE. TIDAL WAVE DAMAGE IS STILL BEING ACCOUNTED FOR. MORE EARTHQUAKES AND A LOSS OF LAND AREA IS EXPECTED.

After the word about the broadcast had passed through the entire boat load of people, everyone was in a quiet state of anxiety with their own thoughts and fears.

There was still some resemblance of a breakwater left at Pender Harbour when they arrived, but when they rounded Daniel Point, Hodgsons, Pearson, Martin and Charles Islands were gone. The Shardom Islands, just inside the entrance, were submerged as well. The south end of Beaver Island, which once connected to the mainland, now let open seas wash through.

Larry was exhausted from the constant working of the sluggish boat as it passed through the now much larger swells, as if the remnants from a large storm at sea had just passed. As they motored around a small peninsula into Garden Bay, they noticed the absence of floating boats, although several vessels were beached above the tide line. Apparently from the high waves caused by the earth's upheavals. For some reason, most of this area had remained above water.

They found only a broken dock at the yacht club. There were seven people there waiting and waving them in. The broken part of the dock had been moved up along side of the remains of an existing section of dock that was intact and anchored to the shoreline. The broken section itself was now blocking the small boat launch ramp. The launch ramp had, at one time, been almost six feet, or better, above the water. Now it was only about six inches above the water's edge and this was at low tide.

On the other side the remaining dock, was the remains of the fuel dock. Its fuel lines appeared to be okay, but the power lines running to it had been ripped away, leaving it useless.

A small tug boat remained tied to the dock just inshore from the fuel dock. Larry moved his boat in along side the broken part of the dock and Ken kicked the fenders, which were still tied to stanchions, over the side to protect the boat from the rough edges of the dock. Then Ken stepped down to secure 'Senseless' to a couple of oversized cleats.

The passengers began to get off the boat and start up the dock toward the others, who had started down to meet them. Larry shut his engines down, and he and Ken were about half way up the dock when the seven men approached them. The rest of the group they had just brought in from the lodge were now waiting at the top of the dock onshore and looking in their direction.

A big burly man approached them saying. "We need your boat to take us to Vancouver Island."

"I'm sorry fella's, but I don't have the time, I have to get some fuel and return to Chatter Box Falls to pick up my wife."

"We don't have time for that. They expect this area to sink under water before long and we've got to get back to Vancouver Island."

"You'll have to take that tug over there then," he said, nodding in that direction. "You're not using my boat."

"We couldn't get the tug to start, so we will be taking your boat." He then pulled a pistol out of his pocket and said, "Take them up to the storage shed and lock them in it."

Larry was not the type to shrink from a fight, as he could normally be pretty aggressive himself. He was also aware there wasn't any way he and Ken could come out on top in this situation. He resigned himself to the loss of his boat. Four others in the group of seven men grabbed them roughly and dragged them up the dock to an empty storage building, threw them inside and locked the door behind them.

Larry and Ken could see out some small holes in the sheet metal siding. They watched the seven men, and the original twenty eight others passing five gallon cans of gasoline hand over hand down the dock. They were putting the fuel into the tanks of Larry's boat. Brian McCormick was at the helm as they backed out away from the dock. "God help them," said Ken.

"What do you mean, God help them. What about us?"

"Larry, you've made the crossing from Nanaimo to Pender Harbour in your powerboat with only the two of you on board. They have thirty five people on that boat. If the seas get any rougher, and I'm sure they will, they may not make it across."

"God, you're right, and anyone who ends up in water that cold is a goner."

After the boat had disappeared around the end of the peninsula, Ken, who had been assessing the condition of the small building they were in, started to kick at the walls of their confinement trying to find a weak spot. "Sorry about your boat."

"Yeah, she was a good vessel, but my insurance should cover her loss."

"I'm not sure your insurance is going to do you much good, considering what's going on."

"You're probably right. Well, let's see if we can find a way of getting back to our wives and friends."

It took them about twenty minutes of hard kicking and prying of loose metal to get out of the shed. After a brief look around the area, they wandered up to the yacht club building. Inside the building they found some food in the yacht club kitchen, and ate heartily.

While they were eating some sandwiches and drinking a semi-cold beer from the refrigerator, Larry said, "Well, partner, it seems we may be in a bit of a fix."

"You may be right. It's getting late though, so let's have a better look around tomorrow and see who, or what, may be left around town. Then we can have a look at the tug boat they couldn't get started, maybe we can find out what's wrong with it."

After they finished eating, Larry found a telephone and lifted the receiver to his ear.

"Anything?" Asked Ken, as he had watched Larry's reaction.

"Dead as a doornail," Larry said.

THE LODGE

Lyn and Theresa were talking quietly in the cockpit of 'Itchy Feet'. The boom tent was over their heads offering them shade and protection from the weather. Helen had just left; she was on her way to her boat to get some special tea she kept aboard. She wanted to treat Lyn and Theresa with some of this tea while the three of them talked. On 'Itchy Feet', Loyd was preparing to leave, and white skin that seldom got into the sunlight was showing as he pulled on a sweatshirt. His thoughts were interrupted when Lyn called down to him.

"Sweetie would you put the tea pot on and heat some water, please?"

"Sure enough, babe."

He lifted the lid off the tea pot painted like a pink pig, then swung the pot under the water spigot in the sink. His foot found the foot pump for fresh water and he pumped until the pot was almost full. Setting the pot on the stove, he got the can out of the cupboard that kept the kitchen matches safe and dry. A small piece of old sandpaper was also kept in the can. A small WWMMMPPHH was heard as the propane ignited, then he set the pot over the flame.

Before leaving he picked up his baseball cap, the name 'Nimitz' adorned the front, and pulled it over his head. It always bothered him to have rain hit him on top of the head. It reminded him of rain hitting a tin roof. He had, over a period of time, gotten in the habit of protecting the bald part of his head from the elements. Leaving the cabin he picked up a small portable hand-held VHF radio.

He worked his way between Lyn and Theresa's feet in the cockpit and climbed out of the cockpit just as Helen returned. "See you ladies later."

Loyd walked to the stern of 'Itchy Feet' and untied a small line holding their dinghy in place. He stepped down into the inflatable, moved to the rear of the small boat and sat near the outboard motor. He primed the engine, pulled the starter cord and the engine came to life with a soft gurgling of cooling water flowing from its exhaust port.

He waved as he left the women sitting in the boat preparing their tea cups with Helen's special tea and eating some cookies Lyn had produced from one of her cupboards. He was heading for the lodge. He wanted to be there where he could see down the full length of the waterway to wait for Ken and Larry's return.

At the lodge, Loyd tied the inflatable dinghy to the end of the dock nearest the main lodge building. He climbed out of the dinghy and onto the dock and walked up the ramp toward the lodge. The place looked deserted. 'Of course it should be,' he thought.

Before he entered the main lodge building, he toured the other parts of the lodge, most were locked. He didn't care what was in them anyway. Returning to the main lodge he turned the knob on the large door and pushed it open. Surprised to find the door unlocked, he entered the lodge listening for sounds of activity, nothing but quiet greeted his ears. Inside the main lodge he found a large room with tables scattered about the room. There were some hard back chairs, what appeared as comfortable couches, and a few stuffed chairs in the room. He walked over to the fireplace and tried in vain to warm his hands by the last embers from an earlier fire.

He thought it strange that there were still a few embers left in the fireplace this late in the day. He walked to one of the large picture windows, which allowed him a full view to the south end of Queen's Reach. While he stood there a quick look told him there wasn't any boat to be seen. Out of curiosity he started looking through this part of the lodge.

At the end of a hallway, off the main room, he opened a door that led into a large, very well equipped kitchen area. He found that the main cook stoves were electric, but there was also an old wood stove for backup cooking in case of a power failure. It was clear to him the kitchen was intended to feed many people at once. Large cooking pots hung in several locations around the walls.

He walked out of the kitchen and to the other end of the hallway. There, a room on the left at the end of the hall, he found a unlocked padlock dangling from the hasp on the door. But, the door was slightly ajar. He pushed it open only to find a small, well furnished bedroom, he closed the door as he left.

Retracing his route, he returned to the south end of the hallway nearest the main lodge room. Looking up he saw other rooms above the main floor, he climbed the stairs to the upper level. On the second floor landing he explored the many rooms. All were bedrooms except for a large linen closet and a storage room. Returning to the lodge's main floor, he went out the same door he had used to enter the building.

His curiosity led him in search of the power supply source for the electrical needs of the lodge. He only had to walk a short distance to the rear of the building. Behind the lodge, Loyd pushed open a door to a well built power shed. It was dark inside and had the familiar odor of oil and fuel. He could make out a large yellowish string hanging down from the ceiling just in front of him, and he knew without thinking what it was, he pulled it. Two small dim lights came on, but they were enough to illuminate most of the building's interior. "Ahh," he said, realizing the bulbs were twelve volt bulbs running off a battery somewhere nearby.

The main occupant of the building was an electrical generator that stood about neck high and about eight feet long. "God, this should just about power anything they would ever need up here," he said to no one. It appeared to be in good condition. He pulled the dipstick out of the engine block and found the oil was up to the full mark. A large ninety gallon diesel fuel tank was mounted at the back of the room on a concrete pad and above the engine's level. The fuel line had a shut off valve, it was turned to the off position.

Satisfied, Loyd returned to the main lodge building and once inside he again looked out the window, over the drained swimming pool, to the south. There was no boat in sight. The fire was out, but the room still retained some warmth. He went over to one of the nearby couches and sat down. He found a Discover magazine on an end table and began thumbing through it. Then he lay down on the couch just to get comfortable, and with his feet now up on the other end, he stretched out full length.

Loyd awoke with a start. Something was shaking his leg, 'My God! What the hell is going on?' His eyes popped open but didn't adjust to the light quickly. He jerked his leg away from whatever it was that was shaking it, and his hearing picked up a voice saying, "You're not supposed to have your feet on the couch, Sonny."

By now his eyes were focusing on the face of a grizzled old man, his gray beard stubble about three days old. By age he appeared to be somewhere in his late seventies or early eighties. "Holy smokes! I didn't know there was anyone around here!" Loyd said automatically.

"There isn't, it's just you and me, but be considerate and keep your feet off the couch."

"Yes sir," Loyd said without thinking, as if he'd been scolded by a parent. Then he added, "Who are you?"

"Name's Hank," he said. Leaving Loyd on the couch, he moved away and went about preparing the fire place for another fire.

As Loyd tried to pry information out of Hank, Hank kept at his task. He laid a bed of small kindling in place on the grate inside the fireplace. It was stacked in a such way that it made a small pyramid, with two small pieces of wood that he had cut with a pocket knife leaving shavings sticking out from each piece of wood. They needed only a match touched to them to start the fire. Progressively Hank added larger and larger pieces to the stack until it was ready to touch a match to it. He did this so the fire would be ready when needed.

Loyd found out that Hank wasn't very talkative, but he did finally tell him he had been hired about three years ago as a caretaker for the winter months and had just stayed on. He still tended the place just to have something to do. His wife and family were long gone, he was alone for the winter months and liked it that way.

THE TUG

The yacht club's guest quarters were comfortable, but during the late evening the electrical power had gone off. Ken had checked the main fuse panels, with a flashlight he had found near the registration desk, and everything seemed in order. During his tour of the building he passed by some windows and he had looked out. It was dark in every direction. He decided the power was off over the entire area. This wasn't really a surprise considering the devastation that had happened in the area. He found his way back to the room that he and Larry had chosen to sleep in, and went back to bed.

The night seemed to stretch on forever and both men spent a restless night. They'd heard strange noises in the night, both of them at one time or another had been up looking around to see what was causing the noises. They had found nothing to pinpoint the source.

Ken was dreaming of a large ice flow bearing down on him at sea, and it was threatening to demolish his boat. This taking place just as he was being shook awake by Larry. As he came out of the groggy sleep state, he heard Larry saying, "Hey, Buddy, we better get a move on if we're going to get anything done this morning."

Ken shook the sleep from his eyes as he twisted around and sat up on the edge of the bed. He only had to slip his shoes on because he'd slept in his clothes with only a blanket pulled up over him. He'd wanted to be ready to move in a hurry if it was necessary.

"Okay, lets do it," he said, as he forced his eyes to adjust to the surroundings.

The sun was bright and warming as they left the front door of the yacht club building. They didn't bother locking the door behind them; they didn't see any need. Keeping an eye out for anyone who might be around the area they worked their way down to the yacht club docks to where the tugboat was moored.

They walked from one end of the tug to the other looking it over, then they climbed aboard. They found what seemed a good sound vessel, nothing had been destroyed and the hull looked good. To their surprise the keys were in the ignition switch on the engine console. Larry reached for the ignition key, turned it and they listened. What they heard was the sound of the engine turning over, however, it was apparent it wasn't going to start.

Ken said. "Larry, I'll get down in the engine compartment and when I'm ready I'll holler at you when I want you to try starting her again. Then while you're try cranking her over I'll have a look to see if I can find out what's wrong."

"Okay."

Ken lifted the engine hatch cover, and with it free he leaned it against the outer bulkhead of the cabin. Easing himself down a short ladder into the space below he found a clean, freshly painted engine compartment. 'A rarity these days,' he thought. When he found a good place to sit next to an air compressor, he settled down. Then he noticed a small overhead light mounted above the forward part of the engine. Pushing the sliding switch to the on position, the small light illuminated the darker areas of the compartment. Then he said, "Okay Larry, give her a crank."

Larry turned the ignition key to the starting position and the engine began to turn over. Still, it would not start. "Hold it, Larry. Let me check something out." Ken then moved to the forward end of the engine compartment. After some searching he found a two-way valve going to the nearby fuel tanks. "Larry, do you have fuel gauges on that panel?" he hollered up.

"Yes, there's only one gauge for fuel but there is a toggle switch that says FUEL #1 on one side of the switch and #2 on the other side. But, the gauge is reading empty. I guess I should have noticed that before, huh?"

Ken sat thinking for a moment mulling the basic fuel system over in his mind. Has to be more to it than just fuel, must be something I've missed. Then a second later he continued, "Switch it to the other tank and see if that makes a difference." A second later he heard the click of the switch.

Larry said. "That did it. The gauge is rising, so we have fuel in tank number two."

Ken turned the valve to the other tank and said. "The fuel valve to the tanks was turned toward the empty tank. That's why they couldn't get her to start. I've turned the other tank on, so give it a try."

Larry tried to start the diesel engine, but it still wouldn't come to life. Ken said. "Hold it a minute, Larry. See if you can find me a tool box up there somewhere."

"Yeah, okay." Ken could hear several of the cabinets being opened and closed, then a couple of minutes later Larry appeared at the engine room hatch with a tool box and said, "Here you go. What gives?"

"I think they compounded their problems with this tug. It's apparent they didn't know about the two tanks or how to change the fuel line from one tank to the other with the two-way valve down here. Then I suspect they sucked air into the fuel injectors from the empty tank and she won't run with air in the injectors. So, what I'll do is bleed them one by one."

"What can I do?"

"You can crank the engine over for me when I holler. What I'll do is remove the fuel line from each fuel injector one at a time. Then I'll have you turn the engine over until we get clean fuel out of that fuel line to that injector. Then we'll repeat the process with each injector down the line until we have the air out of each one of them. Then she should go."

"Okay. Yell when you're ready."

Ken started with cylinder number one. He used a small open ended wrench that fit over the brass fuel fitting and removed the fuel line from the top of the fuel injector. Then with a rag he'd found in the engine compartment placed under the end of the loose fuel line, he called out to Larry to crank the engine over.

It only took a few revolutions of the diesel engine to get clean fuel to the injector. Once the bubbles stopped coming out, and only clean fuel appeared with each stroke of the fuel pump, he told Larry to stop cranking the engine. He then replaced the fuel line onto the injector to cylinder number one. Finished with the number one cylinder he moved to number two cylinder and went through the same procedure all over again. Then on to cylinders three and four until they were all pumping clear fuel. As he moved back to the engine compartment hatch opening, he called out to Larry, "Okay, see what happens now."

Larry turned the ignition key to the start position once again and after just a few revolutions the engine started. It ran a little noisy at first, which is common for a cold diesel, but then the engine began to settle down, growing quieter as it got warmer. After Ken closed the engine hatch he went outside and looked over the side of the tug to be sure there was cooling water coming out of the exhaust pipe with the engine's exhaust as well.

"Good job, Ken," Larry said to him when Ken had returned.

"Tell you what let's do. I'll turn the fuel off again, so no one else can get her to start should they try, then let's go have a look around town. We'll need some supplies and this tug can haul anything we need."

"I think you're right, Buddy. If everyone has abandoned this place, who knows how many other places around here have been abandoned.. We might as well take as much as we can now."

SUPPLIES

Ken and Larry left the tug where they'd found it, tied up at the inoperative fuel dock at the yacht club. Ken turned the fuel off to the engine and Larry had pocketed the ignition keys just in case there might be someone around who might want their newly acquired, and now much needed, tug boat. After securing the boat, they walked back to the yacht club parking lot. Each wandered around independently in search of a vehicle they could use. A few minutes later, Larry hollered, "Hey Ken, this pickup still has the keys in the ignition."

By the time Ken walked to the dark green pickup, Larry had climbed in and started the engine. Grinning, Ken walked around to the other side and climbed up into the passenger seat. "Looks like our lucky day, huh?"

"Well, we know they were in a hurry to leave." Larry put the transmission in gear saying, "And away we go, Pardner."

They drove slowly east around curves, and past small homes, looking for anyone who might be around. Then south and finally west around Garden Bay, up over the hill and down into the central district of Madeira Park. The only city of any size in the Pender Harbour area was eerie with the quiet and lack of people.

"I haven't seen a soul around, Larry. Have you?"

"Nope. Me either."

As they drove down into the lower section of town, Larry commented, "Did you notice the dead crabs and starfish on the ground in the school yard and on some of the lower streets around here?"

"Yeah, seems strange."

A few seconds later. "Hey Larry, there's a hardware store. Lets check it out. Okay?"

Larry stopped the truck in the middle of the street, turned the ignition off and pocketed the keys. They walked to the door of the hardware store and to their surprise, the door opened when Ken tugged at the handle. "My gosh they didn't even lock the door."

"Probably figured anyone wanting in would just bust it open anyway." They began to wander around inside the store independently, picking up anything they thought may be of use and leaving it near the front door. Before long they had axes, three chain saws, gas cans, cases of engine oil for boat engines and outboard motors, and all of the extra rope and nylon line they could find.

"Larry, come're and give me a hand," Ken called out. Larry, a little concerned with what seemed to be an urgent voice, found Ken in the back of the store trying to pull a small Honda electrical generator up the aisle toward the front of the store.

"Hey, good idea. That could really come in handy somewhere along the line."

"I thought so too, and I think I know where we can use it soon. Its even got a little gas in the tank, but I need a hand getting it out of here."

It was fairly easy for the two of them to load the generator into the back of the pickup, which, by now was backed up to the store's doorway, along with all of their other booty. When they finished loading the stuff from the hardware store they drove to the small supermarket and loaded as many cases of canned goods as they could cram into the back of the pickup with all their other stuff.

"I think we should come back and get more before we leave."

"Yeah, we should, the tug will easily carry anything we can put on board."

They made four more trips to and from the grocery store, before they ran out of deck space on the tug boat. By the time they were finished they understood why they had seen crabs and starfish in many places around the lower main part of town. The tide was coming in and the sea was reclaiming the lower downtown part of Madeira Park. Their last trip back to the tugboat was through shallow saltwater flooded streets in the lower areas. Even the launch ramp at the yacht club was under water.

Not wanting to offend others at the lodge, who did not believe in the use of alcohol, they had stored a few cases of beer and wine for themselves down in the engine compartment.

By late afternoon, on the stern of the tug's deck, they had six fifty gallon drums of gasoline and three of diesel fuel. The cases of food, that had been loaded in this area, were now stacked in every space they could find inside the cabin area of the tug. They had used the portable generator to supply power to the fuel pumps at the marina fuel dock.

After some discussion, about the time of day, the two of them decided to stay over at the yacht club one more night in order to be well rested, and to get an early start the next morning. They knew that if they left this late in the day they would arrive at the lodge in the dark. This could be a dangerous time to be wandering around in a boat without local knowledge of the dangers lurking beneath the surface of the water.

Early the next morning, just as daylight was beginning to break, they left the remnants of the breakwater behind. They turned right heading up Agamemnon Channel, which ran along the south of Nelson Island rather than go around it and north to the entrance of Jervis inlet. The two bodies of water meet at Prince of Wales Reach a few miles to the east, so they would take the shorter route.

The large ocean swells were quieter now, however, the horizon behind them did show promise of some weather in the near future. The tug was making good time under the power of her strong diesel engine, her heavy hull helped make the trip fairly smooth. With the VFH radio turned on they listened for any kind of verbal communications. During the trip, they'd heard some garbled one-sided radio traffic, but they were unable to make much sense of it. Something about a volcanic eruption in Northern California.

THE RETURN

Larry and Ken took turns at the tug's helm. Not that it was tiring to steer the tug; it wasn't. They were doing it more for the experience of learning the tug's behavior, and to allow one another some measure of private time to themselves on the return trip.

Ken knew Larry was upset over the loss of his boat 'Senseless' and how he was going to have to explain it to Theresa. All in all, Ken thought he was taking the loss fairly well.

As they traveled, the tug's knotmeter was holding steady at seven knots through the waters of the fjords. They calculated that they would be back at Malibu Rapids by noon, if not a little earlier. "Boy, Larry, with the wind behind us we're making good time," Ken said to break the silence.

"You're right. And, we're not even pushing her hard. But, you know, being a power boater I never really considered weather, or those kinds of things, unless I had a long way to go in bad weather. Most of the time I would just crank up the power to go faster and outrun anything I could."

"Well, when you're in a sailboat you pay attention to those things all the time. It's the difference between making a comfortable trip, or a miserably wet one," Ken commented.

After that brief discussion it seemed as though Larry had forgotten about the loss of his boat. But Ken knew he hadn't. Losing a boat is a very personal affair.

Shortly after they made the left turn from Princess Royal Reach, up Queen's Reach, the last of the three fjords toward Malibu Rapids, they heard a voice on the VFH radio, channel sixteen. "Ahoy the tug, this is Malibu Lodge. Over."

Ken picked up the microphone, keyed the transmit button, and said "This is Ken on the approaching tug boat. Over."

"Ken, this is Loyd. Is Larry with you?"

"Affirmative. All is well here. Over."

"We've been worried about you two. I've been maintaining a vigil with binoculars all day today. We expected you back yesterday." Then he added, "Where's Larry's boat?"

"We'll explain it to you when we get in. Over."

"Okay. I'll meet you in my dinghy after you get through the rapids. Over."

"Okay."

At eleven forty eight they made the right turn and the approach to what was left of the dogleg into Malibu Rapids. Loyd, standing to the right of the Lodge, was waving at them as they neared the entrance. When he saw them, he ran down to the lodge dock, jumped into his dinghy and started the outboard motor. While it idled, he untied his dock lines, then powered out to meet the tug as it slowly picked its way through the beginning of the ebb tide at the rapids.

As Loyd came along-side the tugboat, he threw his dinghy's tow line to Ken on the stern of the tug. When it was tied to a stern cleat, Ken pulled his bow line up so that the dinghy was touching the stern of the tug, and Loyd climbed over the transom onto the afterdeck, crawling through boxes of canned goods and around the drums of fuel.

"Holy smokes! You fellas' must have bought out the town."

Ken grinned and said, "It didn't cost a dime." He started to explain what had happened while they had been in Madeira Park. Plus the surprising news they had heard on the radio on their way out to Pender Harbour with the group from the lodge. Also what they had received on the VFH radio coming back in, and, of what seemed to have happened to the world as they knew it.

The two of them went into the cabin where Larry had already throttled the engine down. They were now just barely moving. He did this mainly to keep the amount of wave action the tug caused at a minimum.

After they talked briefly, Loyd suggested, "I think we should arrange a group meeting this evening at the lodge with all the folks we have up here and explain the events that have happened as we see them." Ken and Larry both agreed.

Larry said, "What say we take the tug back to the lodge dock and leave her tied up there for the time until we decide what to do?"

"Good idea," Loyd said. Then he added, "Out of curiosity, and mostly because I've spent yesterday afternoon and the whole morning here looking for some sign of you two, I've looked the lodge over pretty thoroughly. I think if we have to spend some time up here that the lodge would be far more comfortable than spending any great length of time on our boats. If we were all down here at the lodge, we could act as a team and help each other get through some hard times"

Ken said, "From what we've heard, I think we could be here for a good length of time...possibly even through the winter."

"That wouldn't be bad," Larry said. "We can make a couple more trips to Madeira Park for supplies and the fresh water supply here isn't a problem."

Larry powered the tug along the outside end of the lodge dock. This would leave space for other boats to pull into the dock in front of the tug and still be able to get the tug in and out easily. When the tug was secure, the three of them got into Loyd's rubber dinghy, cast off, and started toward Chatter Box Falls.

On the way Loyd said, "Oh, by the way, there's a crusty old man comes with the place. Name's Hank. Seems he's the caretaker."

"Nobody mentioned a caretaker to us the other day," Larry remarked.

"Well he scared the crap out of me yesterday when I met him."

"Where's he at?" Ken asked curiously.

"Apparently he has one of the back rooms at the lodge, although I haven't seen him today."

As they neared the park's dock, they heard yells of hello to Larry and Ken. Every one knew they were overdue to return. Theresa popped up out of 'Time Out' and was on the dock like a flash waiting for them, with Helen close behind. After hugs and kisses were enjoyed between the two couples, Larry took Theresa's hand and led her down the dock.

Lyn could see tears running down both their cheeks. She knew it wasn't good news. Ken had given her a brief account of the events leading up to the loss of their boat. Then he and Loyd started going from person to person and boat to boat, telling every one about the meeting to be held at six that evening in the lodge. Informing each of them, they could bring their boat, or their dinghy.

About four O'clock that afternoon, Ken and Loyd pulled their boats away from the dock at Chatter Box Falls and headed for the docks at the lodge. Larry and Theresa were on 'Itchy Feet' with Loyd and Lyn. Another mass of boats followed soon afterwards. By six O'clock the docks at Malibu Lodge looked more like a small yacht club.

THE FERRY

Seven kilometers outside Langdale Canada, they encountered a line of cars, motor homes, vans, trucks and trailers, all lined up in single file along the south side of the roadway. As they approached the northern end of this line up, there were people standing nonchalantly out in the middle of the road talking to one another.

Todd slowed to a stop along side of some of them, to ask if there was a problem up ahead. Rolling his window down as he came abreast of the people standing in the road, he poked his head out and said, "Problem up ahead someplace?"

One of the men turned to him and spoke slowly, "Not that I'M aware of, except, the ferry, of course."

Todd became concerned now, and asked, "What's the matter with the ferry?"

A woman standing with them replied, "Nothing wrong with it. Only, that this is the line for it."

The man said, "Oops, gotta go, we're finally moving again."

Todd looked at Beverly. She was shaking her head in disbelief, both of them stunned with the prospect of a very long wait for the ferry. They knew it happened on occasion, but it had never been this bad. The line started moving forward and Todd just waited for the end of the line to pass him, then he pulled in at the back of it.

It took them two days to get to the front of the line waiting for a turn on the ferry. Todd was almost sure he had seen a couple of people sell their spot near the front of the line, then move their car to the back of the line. He was almost certain it was the same people each time, but with different cars. It seemed, to him, they were just rotating cars to sell the spots.

By the time Todd and Beverly got to the ferry landing in their motor home, the end of the line of vehicles waiting for the ferry was almost nine kilometers behind them. Most folks were sleeping in their cars and going to the bathroom where they could. Privacy and pride were now a thing of the past.

One couple arranged for a room at a nearby motel and were renting out their shower for ten dollars a shower, and getting it. Each individual had to supply their own towels, or whatever they needed. Todd and Beverly both heaved a sigh of relief when they finally boarded the ferry.

The provincial ferry crew members were grumbling to anyone who would listen, they wanted to go home and get their own families and to get out of this area. They didn't want to be here working.

ALONE

She had been lying on the top of her bed reading a magazine article that had caught her eye, when she heard the noise from downstairs. Raising to a sitting position on the edge, her feet found her shoes nearby on the carpeted floor. Still fully clothed she walked silently to her bedroom door and opened it slightly. She could hear angry voices downstairs, and her father protesting to whomever it was that was in the house. Her mother's voice was betraying fear.

The men in the kitchen were demanding money from her father and he was explaining he had none. Then she heard two gunshots, a body crashing over a chair and her mother screaming. Then two more shots and her mother fell silent.

She knew from the voices, and the comments, that the men were searching her father's body. Then two of them walked from the kitchen to the front part of the hallway where they stopped. One said, "Go out and get a couple of empty boxes for what food we can find here in the cupboards, then we'll have a look upstairs to see what else we can find."

One of them opened the front door saying, "Okay, be right back." Then he started out.

She closed her bedroom door as silently as she could. Fearing now for her own life, she crossed the bedroom as fast as she could, trying not to make any noise as she moved. Unlocking her bedroom window, she slid it up to the open position. It tried to stick in the old-fashioned window sides, but it did open.

Again she could hear the men downstairs rummaging through the cupboards in the kitchen. Canned goods were being thrown noisily into boxes. With the window open she crawled out, her feet finding the wooden steps of the ladder her father had fastened to the outside wall for her. It was to be used in case of fire, he had explained to her.

In her haste her feet missed the last step but she landed softly on the damp grass of the lawn. Without thinking she ran toward the family's garage at the back of the property. A little over halfway her right foot caught on the garden hose, tripping her. She came down with a thud, the fall knocking the wind out of her. After a few seconds she began to regain her strength and rose to a kneeling position.

The men were now outside the house. She could hear them talking in semi-hushed tones of urgency. She couldn't wait to find out what they were saying. . .she had to move. Not knowing if they had found out, that there had been someone else in the house, she rose to a crouched position and moved as fast as she dared to the safety of the garage. Pulling the side door open, she moved quietly inside the darkness.

Before she pulled the door closed, she could see the flames inside her parents home. It took very little time for the rapid consuming fire, to completely engulf the house. In the darkness her hands found the small ax her father used for cutting kindling for their fireplace. She clutched it to her body feeling some safety in the knowledge she could use it to protect herself if needed. She moved back to the side door she had used to get into the garage, and opened it just enough to see that the men appeared to be leaving.

78

They were leaving for fear of being seen near their deeds of death. The home now totally engulfed in the high reaching flames. She moved to the family car, climbed inside and locked all of the doors. Fear still gripping her, she crowded down onto the floor of the car on the front passenger side. Her sobs' could have been heard by anyone who might have been near. The ax lay on the floor near her.

Later she eased herself up onto the front seat of the car. The kinks in her limbs were easing off, the pain of being crouched on the floor subsiding. She cried herself to sleep not daring to leave her place of refuge. There wasn't anywhere she could go, and there hadn't been any sirens heard in the distance coming to put out the fire. Julie Martin was alone.

THE MEETING

It seemed like a huge group of people, but it was because all of them had gathered in one place for a change. The central room of the main lodge was in fact just about the perfect place for them to meet. The group consisted of twenty-eight adults and six children of various ages seated around the room on a variety of stuffed chairs and couches. Many sat at the small tables and chairs around the room, with three couples sitting on the large stone fireplace hearth.

The children were fidgety and more curious about the building they were in than the meeting their parents were attending. Some older children were given permission to go outside to play or look around, but with strict instructions they were to stay close to this part of the lodge, away from the empty swimming pool, and out of things in general.

Loyd and Ken started a fire in the large fireplace to take the chill off the room. The couples who were sitting on the hearth occasionally had to dodge a spark as it would pop off a piece of burning wood, and against a screen that had been put in placed. There had been ten boats at the Chatter Box Falls park dock, with three boats anchored away from the docks near the falls. Another boat was moored on a buoy at Mc Donald Island. The island lay about half way between the falls and the lodge.

Fourteen boats were now tied to the dock at Malibu Lodge. The docks were crowded, with some boats rafted up to others that were moored to the dock.

When everyone had settled down, Loyd, who had a natural ability to be a leader of men, tapped an empty coffee mug down against the table he was sitting at. Its odd clattering noise attracted everyone and they focused their attention on him.

"Folks, I've met most of you already, but for those I haven't met, I'm Loyd Brown." He turned slightly, looking slowly around the room, then continued. Pointing his right index finger he continued, "This is my wife, Lyn, on my left is Ken and Helen Dougherty, and on my right," he said, turning the other direction, "is Larry and Theresa Johnson." He allowed a few seconds to pass, then began, "We've asked you here this evening because we thought you should be aware of the recent events, as we know and understand them, about the outside world."

"Larry and Ken are the two fella's who went out to Pender Harbour day before yesterday. They made the trip primarily to take the folks that were here at the lodge out to Pender Harbour so they could get back to their families. While they were outside in Pender Harbour, they were met with some very startling surprises. Surprises that we feel you need to be aware of. "

He stopped and scanned the room with his eyes. "Now let me turn this meeting over to Larry, who will fill you in on those events. "

Larry stood, shuffled kind of uneasily, then started. "I want you to understand I'm not someone who generally worries about things, but I'm worried now." He mulled over what and how to explain what he and Ken had encountered, then he just told it the way it happened. How his boat had been taken from him, and how the entire area around Pender Harbour seemed to be in a state of complete disarray

He told about the radio news that he and Ken heard about the meteor that had collided with earth in the south of Texas somewhere and that, apparently there had been others as well. Also, he explained about the devastating events that had taken place around the world afterwards.

He explained some of the potential events that had been forecast for the future because of the meteor impacts on earth. About the possibility that there had been a volcanic eruption in Northern California and how it appeared as if most of the lower end of Vancouver Island seemed to have disappeared into the openness of the sea. Other islands, that could be seen at low-tide, could not be seen at high tide.

When Larry finished, he paused then passed the conversation to Ken. Their audience in the lodge seemed captivated by the enormity of the situation confronting them all. Ken stood, and added some other minor items to finish what the two of them had encountered. During the course of explaining what had happened, and what they had heard, the two men had been interrupted several times to answer questions until everyone seemed satisfied, one couple near the back could be heard arguing.

When Ken and Larry were through speaking and answering questions, Loyd stood once again and said, "Are there any more questions? "

A few seconds passed before a man rose midway back in the group and said, "Loyd, I'm Charles Jensen and seated on my right here is my wife. Mary. We have the sailboat 'Stars'. I'm curious now about where we go from here."

"Charles, I'm not quite sure what you mean. I suppose you can go anywhere you like."

"Please just call me Chuck," he said. "What I meant is, what are you folks going to do at this point? What, if anything, do you recommend?"

When Charles finished, the loud mouthed man, who had been arguing with his wife, stood. "And, who are you to be making the decisions?"

Loyd was silent for a few moments as he gathered his thoughts. He was aware of the responsibility these two men were placing on him. He could either reject the roll he had taken on, or live with it. He chose the latter with some reservation.

"Please don't think that I'm telling anyone what they should, or shouldn't do. Every one of you will have to make up your own minds as to your future.

As for Lyn and I, we're in agreement on this matter. I'm thinking of going back out to see what, if anything, can be found out about the situation in our surrounding area. Plus we are considering, as are Ken and Larry and their wives, spending the winter right here at the lodge. It has every convenience we could possibly need to survive the winter. Then, if this is our final personal decision, perhaps we'll see if we can find the needed materials for a radio antenna we can mount up on top of the walls of the canyon that might allow us to get some news from the outside world. Perhaps even an antenna to transmit or receive from a ham radio as well."

From the back of the room someone asked, "Isn't there a diesel generator for the electric stoves and the heating systems here?"

"Yes there is," Loyd said. "However I'm not sure of its condition, or how much fuel it has available. I feel anyone staying should be prepared for a stay without the benefit of the generator then we won't find ourselves in trouble if it fails. Also, there are several building here, most we won't have any use for. I suggest we only use this part of the compound because it will be easier to maintain for our group."

After a few moments of silence he added, "Also, even though I haven't seen him today, there's an old man comes with the place. His name is Hank. He seems to be the winter caretaker and is knowledgeable about the place and the area around here as well. I understand he's here pretty much year round. So don't be surprised when you come across him or if you see him. Also, don't let him catch you with your feet up on the furniture like he caught me." He heard chuckles around the room.

While others spoke with Loyd, and after some quiet talk between themselves, Chuck stood once again. Loyd said, "Chuck you have something to add?"

Chuck said, "I'd like to make that trip out with you. Also we, that is my wife and I, would be interested in spending the winter here as well. That is, If you'll have us."

"You would be more than welcome to join us. In fact, anyone who would like to stay, can of course stay. We can all chip in together and take care of the wood cutting, fishing, or any other chores that might be required to make our stay easier," Loyd said.

"I think everyone who is interested in spending the winter here at the lodge, should get together with us so we can make some plans," Ken interrupted, adding his comment to the conversation.

By the time the evening was drawing to a close, most of the folks had decided to spend the winter at the lodge. Some would decide after they had further news from the outside world. Ken, Larry, Loyd and their wives had already chosen bedrooms at the lodge to stay in. They had done this earlier in the day when it was quieter, and before the rest of the group began to show up. Chuck and Mary decided at the last minute to find a room that suited them.

The man and wife, who had been arguing, went back to their boat at the dock.

During the early morning hours of their first night at the lodge, Lyn reached over and shook Loyd's arm, saying, "Honey there's somebody out there."

Groggily from deep sleep, Loyd awoke enough to say, "What?"

"I said there is someone out there."

"Out where?'

"I don't know where, just noises somewhere. You're supposed to look, remember?"

"Yeah, okay." He pulled the covers off, sat up on the edge of the bed, reached down and found his socks. After pulling them on, he walked over to the bedroom door, opened it slowly, listening all the while. There was nothing but darkness. He stepped outside the room and felt his way along the wall of their room toward the balcony railing. There was just enough light from the remnants of the fire in the fireplace to make out the shape of the old man adding some wood to the fire, bringing it back to life and muttering to himself. The words were barely audible.

"Dog'gone city folks don't even care if the fire goes out. I should just let it die. Teach them a lesson when they wake up in the morning as cold as it gets." He muttered, unaware Loyd was watching and listening.

When Loyd retraced his steps and crawled back into bed, Lyn said, "You should put some clothes on instead of running around naked, you know? There are other people here."

"Looks like Hank's a night owl. He's stokin' the fire up," he said as he turned toward her, his hand cupping her breast as she moved closer to him.

NANAIMO

When Jim Harrison arrived, he found the remains of two bodies in the remnants of the house. The embers were still smoking in the early daylight hours. The house, for the most part, was gone. The lack of the third body had given him some hope. As he walked toward the back of the property, he knew the garage was his only hope now. Not knowing what to expect he slowly opened the door on the side of the garage. Walking into the building, his eyes began searching the corners of the building for any sign of life. His mind already conditioned to expect the worst.

When he found her she was huddled down out of sight in her folks' car, with the doors locked and in the protective darkness of the garage. He had seen her shoulder over the top of the dashboard when he started to move closer to the side of the car nearest him. Then he knocked lightly on the windshield. Julie screamed. She was still very frightened and afraid the others had come for her. She did not know how much time had gone by. She grew quiet only when she saw it was Jim.

When the car door opened, she flew into his arms, tears streaming down her cheeks. "Jim, oh, Jim! It was horrible! They broke into the house, demanded our food and money. Daddy refused them and they killed him and Mamma. I got away before they knew I was in the house and I was able to get out here to the garage and hide in the car."

Jim had seen this kind of thing taking place over a large part of the area and said, "It's dangerous to stay here any longer, Julie. We have to get away."

"Where can we go, Jim?"

"We can steal a boat and go to the mainland."

Jim finally worked his way around the ignition switch so they could start Julie's folks' car. He backed the car out of the garage and turned to the southwest to begin their search for a boat. They took care to watch for others around them while they were out looking around the waterfront areas. In their quest, they were only finding boats that were either total wrecks, or on the beach in repair yard cradles with little chance of getting them into the water. Finally at a small marine repair yard, across from Newcastle Island they found what they thought might work. As Julie kept a visual surveillance for anyone who might appear, Jim climbed down into the small aluminum boat where he checked the outboard motor and six gallon fuel tank.

He pulled at the starter rope and the engine came to life on the first pull. He assumed the boat must be used for work around the boat yard. Its paint, an ugly green color with splotches of various colors of bottom paint inside the hull, did not seem a color most would choose. A couple of cheap life jackets lay in the front of the boat, and the six-gallon fuel tank was almost full.

"Julie come on. Let's have a look around."

She climbed very carefully into the boat. She was afraid it would tip over with her. "Where are we going?"

"I don't know. We'll know it when we see it"

They motored out through the opening of the small marina and turned to the south. They traveled as far south as downtown Nanaimo, then decided to go back the way they came. Jim could see the community building on Newcastle Island was just above the high water. Apparently the island had sank deeper into the water. They passed by the marina they had started out from and explored to the north of that area. Still, they did not find anything suitable for their needs.

On their way back to the location where they started, Jim was looking into each of the marina slips as they went along. They had passed one long power boat section with covered slips when Jim turned the dinghy around. He slowed the motor so they moved quietly into the long passage between docks. About half way in he took the outboard motor out of gear and let the boat slide easily into an empty berth next to a motorized houseboat. He shut the outboard off and tied the boat to the dock. Then they sat quietly for a few minutes, when they were satisfied there wasn't anyone around they got out of the dinghy.

Jim took Julie's hand, and lead the way to the house boat. He climbed onto the side deck and tried the sliding door. It slid open easily. He climbed inside leaving Julie outside until he was satisfied it was safe. Then he motioned for her to join him. Julie was amazed when she saw the interior.

"Jim, this is a small floating home!"

While Julie had been admiring the uniqueness of the boat, Jim had gone aft to pull the engine hatch open. When he looked inside, he knew instantly why the boat was still here in the dock. The engine compartment was empty. The engines, for whatever reason, were gone. The inside of the boat smelled musty. The kind of musty that only comes from dampness, which suggested that the boat hadn't been used for some time.

"I think we may have just found our place to hide out until we can go across to the mainland."
The next day Jim convinced Julie to stay in the boat as he went back to her folks' home. She only agreed because she didn't think she would be any help to him in his task. It took Jim most of the day to dig the two graves in the back yard of the home and to bury the remains of her parents. He vomited several times as he worked to get their remains into the graves. When he returned, he was filthy and smelled of death. He washed in the cold sea water near the boat. A fresh water rinse was the final task to rid himself of the sorrow he had experienced in his endeavor.

They parked the car as near as they could to their hiding place, and over the next few days they only moved around at night. Julie would carry their empty gas containers as Jim would siphon gas from any source they came across. When they had five containers of fuel, Jim felt they had enough. He couldn't find any outboard motor oil but he did find some light multi-grade engine oil. It would have to do.

Early one morning they made the impromptu decision. It was time to go. There wasn't any wind to speak of and it was slack water. The tide had just finished going out, and had not started its return when they left the safety of the house boat and started on their journey.

With them, they had two life jackets, two coats that could have been warmer, but weren't; some meager sandwiches Julie had been able to put together, a small plastic hand bearing compass Jim found under the lid of the chart table of the house boat and twenty-five gallons of fuel. Jim motored them down to the south side of Newcastle Island, turning to his right between Newcastle Island and Protection Island to its south, then headed in an easterly direction. The narrow, and shallow opening, that once separated the two islands, now much larger and deeper.

They moved easily over the long gentle ocean swells, their destination barely in sight on the other side. When they cleared the eastern side of the Islands Jim cranked the outboard motor up to a higher speed. Even then he knew it would take them a few hours to make the crossing. He hoped the quiet weather would hold long enough. If it did their trip across wouldn't be too bad. He took a compass fix with the hand bearing compass on one of the more prominent points of land across Georgia Straight. He figured that was about where Pender Harbour lay. As they crossed the open water the tide changed and Jim found he could point the bow of the small boat slightly to the southeast and actually maintain a straight line course toward their destination.

SECOND TRIP TO PENDER HARBOUR

With everyone living comfortably at the lodge, except Neil and Sandi Crawford who continued to argue constantly, they only had to make a daily check on the boats at the lodge dock. Project committees had been set up with each group collectively making work lists which provided some work activity for everyone on a daily basis. All of the work being done benefited everyone in some manner.

The work lists were to be rotated weekly so everyone shared in the various work projects at the lodge. This method seemed to be working to the satisfaction of everyone. Some work assignments were assigned permanently to different people who had more expertise in them than others. Even then, the individuals with expertise in any one field found themselves with a list of those who were interested in learning their respective areas of expertise. This provided an ongoing study group, as they were learning how to perform the new tasks as well.

Everyone at the lodge understood, and previously agreed to, a bowl being placed on a table in the main room of the lodge. These lists contained personal items they would like to have if they could be obtained from the Madeira Park stores. The bits of note paper showed up one or two at a time, and the bowl was over flowing. Loyd had retrieved its contents from the table before leaving for Madeira Park. They would be very busy when they reached Pender Harbour as the shopping list was huge. The contents indicated the needs of everyone at the lodge. Even the children had items on the lists. One of the girls had asked for a pony.

Loyd, Chuck and Bill Spencer from the power boat 'Listless' were familiar with the handling of boats with single screws. Loyd, a little unsure of himself with the tugboat, talked to Larry about how the tug handled before they left. When they backed the tug away from the lodge dock, it seemed easy to maneuver, slow to respond at low speed, but easy.

When they got to the end of Queen's Reach, he turned right into Princess Royal Reach and began encountering some chop from the wind as it rushed toward them from the west. The tug pushed through the water without any problem, though an occasional burst of spray over the bow wet the foredeck. They had kept the Honda generator on board and stashed in a corner of the wheel house, but they were going to see if they could find another small portable generator or two in town as well.

Loyd took turns at the helm with Chuck and Bill, so that they would be familiar with handling the tug in case it became necessary at some later time. Though the tug was a heavy vessel, it was a bumpier ride when they turned up Prince of Wales Reach.

The incoming ocean swells were just large enough to make them uncomfortable and kept them on edge in keeping the bow pointed squarely into the swells. Passing the old fish farm to starboard in the cove on Nelson Island, Loyd said, "We might want to check that place out sometime to see if there's anything of value that we could use.

"It's so isolated in there by itself, it could have a generator for auxiliary power," said Bill.

When they approached the remains of the entrance to Pender Harbour, instead of going south around the small peninsula into the yacht club at Garden Bay, they decided to anchor the tug off the main part of town. The chosen location was near the remnants of some private docks at the south end of the bay. Madeira Park had at one time been the central business area, and anchoring here turned out to be a good decision as the wind was much lighter here in the lee of the land.

"I think one of us should stay aboard to keep an eye on things, while the other two are ashore finding what we can that's on our shopping list," said Loyd.

None of them wanted to stay behind, but Bill Spencer agreed to be the one. Loyd and Chuck put the dinghy into the water and cranked the outboard motor to life. They motored slowly to the remnants of the old government dock that had survived devastation from the large waves. The dock was deep in toward the center of the small town and they left the dinghy tied to it. After a short search they found a pickup and were surprised it had small barnacles beginning to grow on the hubcaps. They found the keys over the sun visor. It came to life after a few seconds of cranking the engine over.

By the time they had scrounged around the town, they had four rifles and three shotguns, plus ample ammunition for each of them. As they drove around the area, they found a house with a ham radio antenna attached to one side. Inside the house they found the ham radio, and a twelve-volt adapter, as well. The adapter would allow them to run the radio off twelve volts direct current, or 120 volts of alternating current.

They decided to take the radio and a smaller portable collapsible antenna with them.

The local Radio Shack store had coax cable and they took all of it. They helped themselves to several different types of electrical connectors, some battery powered radios, all the batteries they could find, and Loyd took a lap top computer for himself.

There was a small marine store nearby where they found two twelve-volt, three amp electrical solar panels, out board motor oil and a few other items they thought might come in handy. The pickup bed was filling rapidly, so they took the load of gear they had back to the dock where they left the dinghy. The pickup truck was unloaded, everything being left on the dock. Then they went out to get Bill from the tugboat, leaving everything on the dock unattended.

When they arrived at the tugboat, Bill said, "You guys see anybody around in town?"

Both men looked at him in surprise. "No. We never saw anyone. Why?"

"I'm not sure I did either, but out of the corner of my eye, I saw some kind of movement between a couple of building over there." his fingers pointing up towards some houses on a nearby hill. "Could have been anything really, birds, dogs, who knows?"

"Well, we'll keep our eyes open then."

Chuck used the dinghy to ferry the stuff from the dock out to the tug, while Loyd and Bill went shopping for more canned goods at the local market. While they were in the grocery store Loyd found a hand truck in the rear storage area and carted all the flour, sugar, yeast, salt, bread pans and any other stuff he could think of that you might need for baking out to the truck.

Most of the items on the bottom shelves throughout the store were ruined because of saltwater contamination. The things they were able to salvage were delivered to the dock. Then the two of them set out on another trip for more needed goods.

This time, when they returned, they had another small generator, a great variety of seeds for planting if the time and the need came, a few sacks of premix concrete to help anchor a radio antenna in place, some two inch aluminum pipe, and clothes line wire. The pickup was almost overflowing with more cases of canned goods and a few cases of various wines. It took them almost three hours just to get the stuff loaded onto the tug.

When they were done with the loading, they pulled the anchor and motored the tug over to the Garden Bay Yacht Club fuel dock. They tied the tug along side the dock, and hooked the generator to the power panel inside the fuel dock shed the way Larry had explained it to them. After they started the generator, they filled the fuel tank of the tug, and another fifty gallon drum of gasoline, and diesel fuel into two more drums that they had located in a nearby storage shed.

Before they left the lodge that morning, Larry had suggested they stay in the yacht club at Garden Bay overnight before they returned and they had agreed.

None of them slept very well that night because it seemed so eerie with the quiet in this once well established community. Because of this, the three of them got up and around early. Morning's first light found them at the dock and they were just about to cast their lines off the dock when all hell started to break loose. The dock began to swing back and forth, the pilings it was attached to were also waving back and forth sluggishly.

A crash to their right drew their attention, and they watched an old two story building come tumbling down. Trees swayed as if they would snap the tops right off. Many seconds passed before the rumbling subsided and the three of them were holding onto anything they could with white knuckles showing. "Lets get the hell away from this dock," said Loyd.

"Damn right," the other two said simultaneously.

Not many miles to their south, Glacier Peak, which had been restless, had come to life again. This, after many years of quiet sleep.

The tug boat's engine wasn't quite warmed up when they cast their lines loose and Loyd backed her away from the dock. They kept a lookout aft as they pushed the tug at ten knots up past Nelson Island, just in case they were to encounter a tidal wave caused by the earthquake.

En route to the lodge they monitored the VHF radio and heard only static.

SOUTH DAKOTA

"Well, Margi old girl, I just finished splittin' the last'a the load of wood we cut a week ago tomorrow, an' it's all stacked up neat like.

How much wood we got now?

"Bout fifteen cord, I'd spose."

"Are we gonna need that much wood?"

"Probly not, but it feels a bit like a tough winter comin' on. . . .Least that's what my bones are a tellin' me, an the woolly bear caterpillars are showin' it too"

Margaret had spent many days canning meat and vegetables this past summer, and their larder was well stocked. The canning of food products was the way she had been raised as a girl, and now it was more of a habit than anything else. The two of them had lived here near the lake in their small two bedroom home since they had married many years before. They knew how to survive tough winters, and they had put in quite a few of them over the years here at the cabin. It had become a habit more than anything, but they were always prepared for tough winters.

As a last minute thought she said, "Moe did you get the boat put up for the winter yet?"

"Yep. Put it up on saw horses under the lean to along side the guest house."

They'd built the small guest cabin several years ago for their son and his family. It allowed them to have some privacy while the children were here visiting, yet they could still visit with them any time as well. It also gave the older folks some quieter visiting time in the evenings after the grandchildren had been put to bed in the cabin.

ANTENNA

When the three men returned to the lodge from
Pender Harbour, they learned that the earthquake they
had experienced on the outside had done little more
than shake them up at the lodge. The lodge itself
hadn't suffered any damage.

Two days after they returned to Malibu Lodge, Loyd,
Ken, Larry, and Frank Bowen had gathered their
antenna supplies together and set out early in the
morning. The group of men had ropes for climbing and
hauling their materials up the rocky slopes slightly to
the north and east of the lodge. They carried lunches
Aireanna had made for them, under the supervision of
the other women in the kitchen. They also had the
antenna they had confiscated in town with them and its
related gear.

In the past Frank had been a ham radio operator in his
hometown and he took on the responsibilities of being
in charge of their communications operations. It had
been his suggestion about where they should place
the antenna for the best possible chance of sending
and receiving radio transmissions. This decision had
been influenced partially because of the limited length
of coax cable they had in their possession and the
nearness to the old McDonald cabin.

It took all morning for the four of them to climb to the
top of the chosen rocky crest. It would have gone
quicker and smoother had it not been for the four bags
of concrete mix and the containers of water to mix it
with. The trip up the side of the rocky terrain had
required them to move the concrete slowly to keep
from tearing the ninety-four-pound bags open and
losing the contents. The water that was to be used in

mixing the concrete was in somewhat pliable containers and even though they were cumbersome, they traveled well. An empty five-gallon plastic water jug with the top cut off was more a nuisance to carry along, but it was to be used to mix the concrete in.

The day before the climb, they pre-built the antenna by drilling holes through the bottom of it and through one end of a two inch pipe the antenna was to be fastened to. The two pieces of pipe were to be joined by a threaded nipple. They also drilled holes for guy wires in both pieces of aluminum pipe.

On reaching the top of the rocky ledge, their chosen location, they all sat down winded. They rested as they ate their lunches. Shortly after they had eaten lunch and were just chatting, Loyd said, "We better get this thing up, hadn't we?"

Frank, who had been walking over the area and looking around while he ate his lunch said, "I think this is the best spot for the antenna." He pointed to a nearby hole in a rock.

"We should have enough coax to reach the cabin from here." The cabin stood by itself less than a quarter mile from the main lodge, and just northeast of McDonald Island. It was thought that at one time it had belonged to Mr.James McDonald himself, though his main home had been near the waterfall. The lodge's staff over the years had maintained this cabin, keeping it in excellent condition.

In just a few minutes the antenna was assembled and ready to hoist into the air. Loyd and Ken had been digging holes where Frank had indicated he wanted them. These holes were areas where dirt had been removed from between two or more large rocks. Larry cleaned out the hole where the base of the antenna was to sit, and was in the process of mixing concrete for filling the hole around the base of the pipe when it was set in place.

Frank, putting last minute touches to the antenna, used an ample supply of electrical tape to secure the coax cable to the side of the pipe to avoid abrasion of the cable. He had already screwed the two pieces together and fastened the antenna to the top piece of pipe using three of the nine nuts and bolts they had brought along.

Two more bolts were pushed through two holes in the base of the bottom pipe to act as an anchor when the concrete had set up around it. The remaining bolts would be used as anchors at the ends of the eight guy wires which were also going to be set into concrete.

"Okay, is everyone ready?" Frank asked. He received a positive reply from everyone. He had them all assemble at the base of the antenna, and they pulled it up into the air and into place. When it slid down into the hole in the rock, Larry started mucking in some of his wet concrete mix. With this done, they placed large rocks around the base to help support the antenna until the concrete set up and these were mucked together with concrete as well.

Ken and Loyd held the antenna upright while Frank and Larry went around arranging the guy wires with the remaining bolts setting them all into their respective locations. With the guy wires finally set in concrete they placed large rocks on top of each to help keep them in place until all the concrete was set. It would set up quickly, but would take a few days for the concrete to cure completely. When they were finished, they had an antenna that stood just over twenty feet above ground level at the chosen location on top of the rocky crest. Frank planned on returning in a few days, after the concrete set up, to make any adjustments needed to take up the slack in the guy wires. His plan was to put a stick between the ends near the base to twist it like a tourniquet.

It was nearly dark by the time they had unrolled the coax cable back down the side of the rocky hillside covered with scrub brush. Any connection to the cable would be heavily taped to save them problems with corrosion at a later date. The cable had been tied loosely with heavy wire ties at many locations along the way down the slope as well. Once the end of the cable was at the cabin, it would be up to Frank to get the radio operational. He'd confiscated the solar panels they had found at the Radio Shack Store to keep his two twelve-volt batteries at full charge for the radio.

Kerosene for his lamps in the cabin were kept in four five-gallon containers in a lean-to next to the cabin. The wood cutting crew would keep him and his wife Jessie supplied with firewood at the cabin as they needed it. This had been agreed upon by everyone at the lodge so that Frank would be excused from all other duties and he could then maintain a constant radio watch. Frank enjoyed the solitude of searching the airwaves. He was like a detective searching for clues.

He explained to the group one evening that sometimes the best radio transmission could be in the middle of the night, or late evenings. "You just can't tell when it's going to be a good time to send and receive, but the later hours are usually the most productive."

WINTER PREPARATIONS

The group continued getting together for weekly meetings at the lodge. The discussions lately were directed more toward needed preparations for the upcoming winter. Everyone now aware the fireplace consumed a great amount of firewood to keep the whole lodge warm all the time. They had talked over several solutions, but finally decided in order to keep the need for heat distribution at a minimum, all the doors to the unused rooms should be kept closed at all times.

Most of those who had bedrooms upstairs were leaving their doors open during the day, this allowed the rising heat of the day to penetrate their rooms to warm them. A few, who liked to sleep in cooler rooms, had taken downstairs bedrooms. Some like Loyd and Lyn kept their upstairs bedroom door closed during the day to keep the rising heat out of their rooms and often slept with the window open at night as well.

This arrangement worked well, as most of the downstairs bedrooms had been converted to storage areas for the group's food supplies. Other supplies, like the drums of fuel and oil, were stored in a small building a short distance from the lodge.

Hank's room was the only exception. His room, the only one with a padlock on the door, was at the end of the hall. Hank locked his room whenever he left the lodge. He learned over a period of time that he didn't have to lock his door with this group of people, most folks just thought it was something that carried over from his younger years.

Hank had somewhat of an odd nature. Few of the group at the lodge understood him, but knew he was getting up at night to keep the lodge fires going. Yet, because of his age, his wishes were given respect and no one ever questioned him. Even when they asked him questions, they rarely got answers. No one ever entered his room even if it was unlocked.

Some large tarpaulins had been spread over the floor of one of the larger rooms downstairs to protect the floor from dripping water. This room had been chosen as a clothes drying room. Personal laundry was done in the lodge's laundry facilities in cold water. On days designated as 'laundry day' and when there were many loads of wash being done, this room was used to hang laundry on the many clotheslines that had been stretched from wall to wall. This was done to keep from using more of the generator's power than was actually needed. In the end this helped save diesel fuel for the generator.

This was one of the few things at the lodge that Sandi Crawford used as well. Neil had insisted that the two of them stay aboard their boat at the dock. Sandi had been seen with bruises on her arms and though she blamed herself for them, everyone at the lodge was sure Neil was tough on her. Even during the night you could hear an occasional argument coming from their boat. They had, in a sense, become recluses from the rest of the group.

On one of the first days of wood cutting Loyd and Bob Franklin were standing on the east side of the lodge talking together about the amount of wood they thought would be needed for the coming winter months.

"How much wood you figure we'll need, Loyd?

Well, it might be kind'a hard to figure, but when we lived in the high Sierra Mountains, we used about five cords of wood each winter to heat just under fifteen hundred square feet of house. Course that was a fire going almost constantly from October or November through to about March or so. We used oak which will burn very slowly so the fire would last quite awhile."

Bob said. "Tell you what. Suppose I take over the wood cutting crew permanently and we'll cut at least five cords of wood for each family."

"Okay, works for me. We'll tell the group at the next meeting and see if they agree to that arrangement."

Later in the day as Loyd walked around the east side of the lodge, he saw Bob bending over, measuring out an area with a rope. He stretched it out between him and one of the children. Then a couple of the other children would pound stakes into the ground where Bob indicated.

"What're you building Bob?" Loyd said, a little amused.

"Hum, oh." he looked around. "This is the size of the wood pile we'll need."

"Holy smokes! That big?"

"Yep. It's thirty feet by forty feet. It's actually larger than what I think we'll need, but better safe than sorry."

"It'll keep your wood cutting crews busy trying to fill it," Loyd said as he surveyed the large area.

"I s'pose. But they're already starting to see which wood cutting crew can out do the other. They've got one bunch cutting rounds off the fallen trees, and some more who're splitting the cut rounds up. Then some who are transporting the wood back here."

"Sound like they're pretty efficient."

"Yeah, and with that kind'a attitude, I'm thinking they'll probably fill this wood spot up fairly quick."

"You're a good man, Bob," Loyd said, patting Bob on the back of the shoulder as he was leaving. "See ya."

"Yeah, later." Bob turned back to his work.

Some of the groups on wood detail had been very inventive in finding wood supplies, as they didn't want to cut any live trees if it was possible. They were picking up any dead wood or windfall trees in the forested area around Chatter Box Falls. Trees that had fallen off the sides of the rocky precipices were hauled one at a time with a dinghy and an outboard motor down to the lodge dock area and pulled ashore with a large old block and tackle that had been found in the diesel generator building. Then it was cut up with chain saws.

One enterprising group was keeping a watch out toward the open water area outside of Malibu Rapids for floating logs. When weather permitted they would use a couple of dinghies to go out after them.

Sometimes they would have to leave a log or two out in the fjord tied to a rock or tree on shore until it was slack water at the rapids so they could be towed inside to their cutting area.

On occasion the cutting crews would venture across the waterway to the far shore, or up and down the shoreline in search for logs they could wrangle into the water and back to the lodge. Logs that had been in the salt water any length of time were a problem for the chain saws. They dulled the cutting teeth of the chains very quickly. This would keep someone busy just sharpening the cutting teeth on the saws, but wood was wood and they had a spot to fill up.

Frank had finally gotten the ham radio in operational condition and was putting in long hours every night trying to establish contact with anyone. The cloud conditions were erratic so bouncing the radio signal off the cloud cover just wasn't working and he was concerned. He was afraid his antenna might be just high enough that perhaps the transmit signal he was putting out might be going right over the top of any other antenna in this part of the country when he transmitted anything on the air.

He had heard some informative reports on occasion. Those that he'd been able to listen to said there had been recent volcanic eruptions in several places world wide. Two volcanoes were now spouting in California, he thought they had said Mt. Shasta and Lassen, two more in Oregon which were Mt. Hood and Three Sisters, Mt .St. Helens and Glacier peak in Washington, plus one was spewing steam on the Washington coast, or what had been the Washington coast. There was one in Japan, a new one in the

Hawaiian Island group and someone had said something about a new island off the Columbia river basin on the Oregon coast.

Apparently the volcanic activity was believed to have been caused by tectonic plates collapsing. It seemed the asteroid's impact had affected all plate activity. Frank, himself wasn't dismayed about not having made personal outside contact. He was receiving news on occasion and knew he would make contact at some point, it was only a matter of time.

At the lodge, everyone enjoyed it when Lyn made salad for an evening meal, which was a rare treat. Most often her salads would contain some kind of wild greens she had found nearby and often fresh sprouts as well. Little did they know Lyn had a large supply of sprout seeds stashed on her sailboat, 'Itchy Feet'.

The group would celebrate one of their more successful days with a bottle of wine for dinner as Loyd, Bill and Chuck had seen fit to liberate several cases from the grocery store on their last visit to Madeira Park. It seemed that Hank, on occasion, would seem a little tipsy. They figured he had his own supply of liquor hidden somewhere. Nobody knew where, nor did they care.

The lodge generator was only being used to supply power for the cooking stoves during the hours they needed to cook meals and the hot water heaters.

Other than that, they were turning it off to conserve the fuel supply. A few men at the lodge were successful in their efforts at deer hunting and had been doing some hunting up and down the whole of the Queen's Reach area. Because of their success they frequently dined on fresh venison.

One evening during the meal, Tony and Marie Barton were sitting with Loyd, Lyn, Ken, Helen, Larry and Theresa, when Tony said, "You know we ought to build a smokehouse for some of this venison."

Loyd was surprised at the simple solution. After he finished swallowing a bite of food, "That's a damn good idea, Tony. Do you know how to build one?"

"Well, I haven't actually built one myself, but my grandfather used to smoke his venison every year. So I'm aware of how they work and about how they're put together."

"What's a smokehouse?" asked Larry. His mind envisioning a large old Indian lodge building of some kind.

"It's a small shed built over a pit, this pit is connected with a large pipe to another pit somewhere nearby. The shed is where you hang the meat you want to cook with hot smoke, and the other pit is where you keep a fire, of hardwood chips smoldering. This way you can keep the meat for a later time when there's no game around.

"We could smoke fish in it as well," mentioned Ken.

"Tony, what do you need to build one of these things?" asked Loyd.

"I've been thinking about this for a little while now, and I started looking around a couple of days ago. It

111

seems to me that we have everything we need to put one of these together. If you could let me have the older children for a few days, to haul rocks for the foundations of the pits, I could build this thing."

"You can't have Aireanna," Lyn said quickly. "She's been helping us in the kitchen and I'm getting ready to hold classes on bread making. Aireanna wants to learn how to do this so I'm keeping her with us in the kitchen." She didn't bother telling them she kind'a favored Aireanna. She didn't have to tell them this, they already knew it.

"I understand that the boys John, Randal and Robbert are assigned the task of splitting fire wood and keeping the wood pile topped up for Frank and Jessie over at the radio shack as well."

"Umm. Okay, it looks like I better ask for some help at the next weekly meeting,"

"You can probably get the other two older kids, Tommy and Elizabeth to help and we'll help when we can," Loyd said, his hand sweeping around the group volunteering the bunch of them.

"Oh, thanks," Ken and Larry said together in mock misery.

"One more thing," Ken spoke up, "Frank has taken over maintenance of the lodge generator as well. He's apparently made peace with Hank on the generator's care, but Hank looks in on it on occasion as well. Frank says that there may or may not be enough fuel for the winter in the tanks, but he would feel better if we topped them up before then."

"We better make another trip out to Pender Harbour for some more diesel fuel then, and the sooner the better," said Loyd.

"I'll go with you," said Larry, "if it's in the next couple of days." Then he added, "Not that my personal calendar is full."

"How about day after tomorrow?" asked Loyd.

"I'm going with you this time," Lyn said. "There are some things us gals have been needing."

"We can get you whatever you need," Ken added.

"Lyn will go with you and get our stuff," Helen quipped. A dish water blond whose eyes changed colors with her moods, "Don't argue with us."

"Okay, okay," Ken said, knowing it was time to let it alone.

NEWCOMERS

The trip out to Pender Harbour had been uneventful. Water conditions were quiet and the incoming ocean swells were long and gentle. Only the empty fuel drums they had tied in place on the stern of the tug could be heard on occasion rubbing against one another. When they arrived in Pender Harbour they moored the tug to the fuel dock in Garden Bay. Loyd and Larry were busy hooking up the portable generator to the fuel pump's electrical panel in the fuel shed. Lyn had taken the pickup truck the group had come to call "Our pickup" into town for the things she, and the other women at the lodge, had wanted.

The fella's warned her to keep an eye out for anything that might be of danger to her, but because of the fact that they had not actually seen anyone around when they had been here last, they felt she was safe. Plus Loyd had given her a portable hand held VHF radio to carry with her. It was understood that, if she needed any help she would call them on channel sixteen. They would monitor that same channel on the tug's VHF radio.

When Lyn returned about two and a half hours later, Loyd, who had been apprehensive about her being gone in this area alone said, "Did you get the things you needed?"

"Yes, but I'll need you guys to load it on the tug for me because there are several cases." Lyn had taken every case of canned milk, canned cream, butter, margarine, eggs, Vaseline, every feminine item she came across, plus many items she no longer used, but she knew that someone else at the lodge would. "I used a hand cart at the store and I brought it along."

"Well, why don't you just load it on the boat as well?" said Loyd, teasing her.

"Honeeyyy," she said smiling sweetly. Then added, "Okay I'll bring the small stuff down."

"That's okay, babe. We'll get it for you."

"Guess what else?"

"What else," he said. He never knew what this saying of hers was going to produce.

"Did you know there's still some old people around here?"

"What? Where?"

"Oh, I couldn't tell where they are, but I saw two old women and an old man carting stuff in a wheelbarrow up the hill on the southeast side of town."

"Did they say anything to you?"

"No. I called out to them, but they hurried away and disappeared. And one more thing. "On my way back here, I went sight-seeing. There's a road that goes out to the point of land on the north west end. When I went around the turn just before the end of the road, I stopped and got out to look at the view. While I was standing there, I thought I could hear a small outboard motor in the distance. I'm not sure, but I thought I could see a small open boat heading up this side of Nelson Island."

"Any idea where it came from?" asked Larry, who stopped what he was doing, now more interested in what Lyn had said.

"As far as I could tell, it looked like it came from across Georgia Straight," she remarked.

"My God, that could have been one hell of a trip in a small open boat. We'll keep an eye out for it on the way back to the lodge."

Once the cases of items Lyn had gotten in town were stowed away, covered with a plastic tarpaulin, and the drums of fuel were lashed down tight on the stern deck of the tug, they quit for the day. That night they slept well, even though it was cold in the yacht club building. Loyd always slept well when he was with his wife.

They were in a hurry to get started next morning, so while the tug's diesel engine warmed up they drank a soda pop and stuffed a few crackers in their mouths as they made the preparations for leaving on the tug. After they finished the meager meal, they cast their lines loose from the fuel dock and slowly motored out of the bay.

The rocky breakwater, and land spit, that at one time surrounded a portion of the bay's entrance on the west side, was now little more than an underwater reef. At high-tide the incoming ocean swells rode right over remnants of the breakwater and made most of the bay an uncomfortable place to be. This happened even though most of the wave's energy was spent when it met the remnants of the breakwater, especially in rough stormy weather.

The only quiet water area to be found was back in the northern part of the harbour near the yacht club, or, at the southern end of the bay near the main part of town. The southern end seemed more protected from southwest high winds as well. Some winter winds often blew hard across the bay from the small gorge to the east.

Just under an hour after they cast off from the dock in Garden Bay, they were motoring slowly past the old fish farm building nestled back in an open cove on the south east side of Nelson Island. Lyn's curiosity had kept her looking and now she pointed toward the floating docks and buildings of the fish farm saying, "There's that small boat I told you guys about yesterday."

Loyd knew Lyn wasn't going to let them go by here without looking for whoever it was who came across from Nanaimo in the boat, so he said, "Larry, turn in there, and I'll take a bow line with me when you put our bow up against the dock."

"Okay, but keep an eye out for anything unusual."

"You bet."

Larry slowly maneuvered the tug as he approached the deck close to where the small boat was tied, and Loyd easily stepped down onto the floating dock. When Loyd had the tug tied off to the large deck, surrounding the two story building, Larry left the tug boat's engine running while he joined Loyd. The two men walked slowly up to the wooden building to have a look around.

Lyn stayed on board the tug to keep a watch over things. The two men took their time looking through the downstairs area of the building. Frequently calling out, "Anyone here?" But they didn't receive an answer. Without finding anyone downstairs they had gone upstairs to search. Loyd, in one room, heard Larry in another room say, "Whoa, don't shoot for Christ's sake."

Then a strange excited male voice said, "What do you want?"

Larry hurriedly explained to the younger man how Lyn had seen his small boat come by Pender Harbour yesterday. Also, he quickly explained that the three of them were curious about where the boat had gone, mainly because they hadn't seen any other human beings in this area in the past few weeks.

When Loyd poked his head around the edge of the doorway, he saw a nervous young man with a pistol aimed at Larry and a frightened young woman behind him. The two young people were standing inside a large closet with the door open, and facing Larry, who, when opening the door had found them hiding inside.

"Go easy folks," Loyd said quietly and reassuringly "We're not here to hurt you."

"How do we know that?" the young man in the closet replied. "Hang on just a minute," Loyd said, then he walked over to an upstairs window and opened it. He stuck his upper body out of the window and waved his hand until he caught Lyn's attention. When she came out of the tug's cabin area, he called out, "Lyn can you come up here for a minute?"

118

In a few seconds she came up the stairs and found the fouriome waiting for her. Immediately sensing the tension, she only paused a moment, then she walked over to the closet door and said, "Hi, I'm Lyn, are you two hungry? I could make you some lunch if you like."

This caught the four of them totally off guard, but it diffused the situation immediately. The young woman said, "Yes, I am hungry." She too seemed more at ease now, and after a slight hesitation she continued, "My name is Julie Martin and this is my boyfriend, Jim Harrison."

"Well, come on Julie and we'll find something for you folks to eat." Without waiting Julie followed Lyn out of the room, Jim only hesitated a moment before he followed the two women. He stuffed his pistol into a jacket pocket as he followed Julie and Lyn down the stairs and outside.

Larry and Loyd just looked at each other in awe, shrugged their shoulders and followed the others. Once they were back on the tug, and while Lyn was fixing sandwiches, she asked Julie how they ended up at the fish farm. She and Jim explained how they had hidden for a week and a half in a small houseboat, then in a storage shed near the water in Nanaimo.

They went on to explain how Jim's folks had disappeared without a trace three weeks ago and her folks had been murdered almost two weeks ago for their food supply. She explained how it was chaotic on the island with people just trying to survive. Jim told how they had gone out at night, and in the early morning hours, to steal gasoline wherever they could find it for their trip across to this part of the mainland.

They had started out with about twenty gallons of fuel for their outboard motor, a couple of life jackets and warm coats, but food was scarce.

Loyd asked, "What're your plans for the future?"

"We don't really have any immediate plans. We just thought we would have a better chance to live over here than on the island," Jim added.

"Jim, we have a nice group of folks up at a lodge at Malibu Rapids. We're spending the winter there. If you two would like to join us, you're welcome," Larry said.

"Oh Jim, let's do," Julie said, excited about being with a safe group of people.

"Okay." He glanced around at the four of them. "Okay, we'll give it a try," he said.

"Okay Jim. Tie your boat up to the stern of the tug and let's get a move on," Loyd said, indicating the rear of the boat.

The small boat was trailing aft of the tug, its outboard motor tilted up to keep it from dragging in the water. Larry started moving the tug out away from the fish farm dock, then upstream toward the lodge. Loyd had glanced aft, and noticing some movement taking place with their drums of diesel fuel, he went back to secure them. After a few seconds Larry said, "Jim come take a turn at the helm while I give Loyd a hand tying the fuel oil drums down on the after deck."

"I'm sorry, but I don't know how."

"It's okay, give it a try. Lyn'll keep an eye on how you're doing."

Jim took the brass wheel in his hands saying, "Okay, but don't get excited if I'm all over the water with this thing."

When they were through securing the drums down, Jim was having such a good time steering the tug, they let him continue. Julie just beamed with pride for Jim. About half way back to the lodge, Jim said, "Julie."

She walked over to Jim and said, "Yes?"

He reached into his jacket pocket, fished the pistol out of it, and handed it to her. Julie took it with her thumb and forefinger, holding it as if it was something dirty. "What do you want me to do with this?"

"We won't need it now. Get rid of it okay?"

Julie walked carefully out of the cabin area of the tugboat, still clutching the pistol between her finger tips. Then she went over to the edge of the rail, where she dropped the gun into the cold sea water.

They were nearing Queen's Reach when they saw a sailboat under power heading outward bound. Larry spotted it first, "Hey, lookie here." His fingers pointed ahead and to the port side.

"What's going on?" Now they were all looking at the sailboat as it passed them by.

"It's the Wave Runner, Neil and Sandi's boat."

"I wonder where they're going?" Loyd said.

"Beats me, but it'll be quieter around the docks until they get back."

That night at dinner in the lodge Jim and Julie were introduced to the rest of the group. Most were curious and asked them questions about how it was outside of this area. After dinner, Jim and Julie related how they had survived and how tough it was to live on the island. Some of the news they related to the group was startling and harsh.

One discussion brought to light was that Frank had gotten involved in a heated argument with Neil about his treatment of Sandi. When asked about it, Jessie volunteered the information.

"Frank told him to leave her alone, or he'd whup him good just to give him a taste of his own medicine. Frank was ready, when Neil took a swing at him but missed, and Frank knocked him on his butt. That ended the fight, but Neil started getting verbal with Frank, and Frank told him, "You either behave yourself or get out and don't come back."

Later in the evening there had been some concern between some of the older folks about whether Jim and Julie should share the same bedroom. After some discussion between the group, which did not include Jim and Julie, it was decided to leave things as they were. This was a new time and there was no place for some old outdated beliefs contrary to what one or two others thought.

The next morning found Lyn giving Aireanna instructions on what she was to do with all the eggs in every carton on the table before she put them away. "You take a jar of Vaseline, set it here on the table," she said pointing to an area on the table where she put one of the Vaseline jars down. "Dip your fingers into it like this."

She put her fingers into the small jar of gooey light yellow Vaseline pulling some out of the jar. Picking up an egg, she continued, "Then rub a light coating all over each and every egg. Then put them back into the carton when you're through.' She placed the finished egg back into the carton, then wiped her hand off on a towel she had supplied to Aireanna for this purpose.

"Why do we have to put this stuff on the eggs?" Aireanna asked.

"Cause if you look really close you can see the eggshell is full of real tiny holes and air can get into the egg through those holes. Then the egg will spoil."

"This stuff plugs up the holes, huh?"

"You got it. Also, every couple of days I want you to turn each egg carton over."

"Really?"

"Really. Do you know anything about chickens?"

"No."

"Well, a hen turns her eggs over everyday, that's how she keeps them fresh until they're ready to hatch."

123

"Really?"

"Really. She smiled as she turned away, she liked this girl.

Then, as Lyn walked away, she heard Aireanna say to herself, "Uukky," as she got the first bunch of Vaseline on her fingers. It took her all morning to do the eggs and two towels were covered with the Vaseline she had wiped off her hands.

The next few weeks found the Malibu Lodge group very busy fishing, hunting and using the newly constructed smokehouse on a constant basis. Tony had dug a hole in the ground about three feet deep, then he covered the bottom with rocks. This part of the smokehouse finished, he constructed a foundation of stones, using mud as mortar. The foundation was about three feet high and two feet or so thick and included four support posts on the corners that were to be used for the wooden shed construction on top, with an opening in the side nearest the rocky hillside to the north.

On the top of this foundation he had built a small wooden shed whose door extended from the top of the shed to the bottom of the rock foundation. Inside were some metal rods that extended from one wall to the other to be used for hanging the meat while it was being dried and smoked for preservation. Tony and Marie were on a constant vigil just keeping a smoldering fire going in the pit and they had been excused from all their other previous duties. Meanwhile the winter firewood piles had grown to such an extent that when the area assigned for the firewood was full, even the deck area around the lodge was almost covered in firewood. This made it easier for whomever was tending lodge fires, but they were encouraged to use the wood from the large wood stacking area farthest away. This was to save the closer wood for the winter months when they would have snow, and walking with an arm load of wood would be more of a risk.

Hank, of course, at night had just been picking his wood for the fireplace off the stacks around the deck area. During the day someone from the wood crew would replace the wood Hank had used during the night. They decided it would be easier to put a pile of wood inside near the fireplace for Hank's exclusive use. That way, at night Hank wouldn't even have to go outdoors to get wood for the fire and this way some of the older children were assigned the task of keeping this woodpile supplied as well.

STORM

It wasn't long before most of those in the large room of the lodge had gathered at the lodge windows in wonder. It seemed as though the massive lightning storm was coming right up the Fjord toward them. Comments were flowing freely between them about the spectacular sight they were observing.

Sheet lightning would start in one location, then travel long distances before touching down at another location. Though it only lasted a second or so each time, the light from the lightning was awesome in its blue-white brilliance. The lodge windows would rattle as the booming of the thunder arrived with each concussion of sound as it traveled. The seconds between the flash of light and the booming thunder growing shorter as the center of the storm drew nearer to the lodge.

As a tall pine tree just to the south of the lodge took a hit from a lightning bolt, it exploded just above the ground. Someone, in the back of the group said, "Well there's more fire wood for us." A couple of others chuckled with him but they were awed by the experience of seeing the power of Mother Nature.

Finally the storm front moved on toward the north and away from them. After the storm front passed them by, the group started moving farther back inside the lodge and returning to the events their previous events. A 'clunk, clunk' could be heard as someone added more wood to the fire in the fireplace.

Outside, in Queen's Reach, the waves were building with the heavy wind as it raced along with the storm front. Less than a mile from where the waves reached their highest peak, they crashed against the shoreline. Rocks were rolled like bowling balls offering very little resistance to the water's need for their space.

DETOUR

Todd and Beverly's trip had been going well, but the weather had been growing worse daily, and today it was getting worse by the hour. They were traveling cross country on Highway 90, but when they reached Mitchell in South Dakota, they encountered a road block. The highway patrol officer stationed there instructed them to take Highway 37 north. This would take them around the area of the highway that was blocked by a seventeen car pile up just up ahead.

The day seemed to be an extra long one, partially because they had stopped to put their chains on, then had to drive slower to keep the chains from beating against the inside of the fender wells. They were both hungry and tired, and the strain was showing in their conversation. The falling snow had been coming down steadily and heavily for almost two hours. A few miles after they turned north on Highway 37, Beverly saw a sign advertising home cooked meals just ahead. She made the suggestion, "Todd why don't we stop there for a bite to eat?"

"Good idea Honey," and he began to slow down for the intersection. They turned east off the highway and wound their way down a back country road. Following the small signs, they were lead to a very small roadside café with a gravel parking lot set back off the pavement. A farm tractor, fitted with a front loader bucket used to clear the parking lot was parked off to one side.

Inside the café they found a plump elderly woman wearing an old and worn apron, also a thin old man who walked with a limp. His bib coveralls hung loose on his body. Todd and Beverly sat at a table near a small pot belly heating stove, looked at the hand-written menu, and ordered when the elderly woman approached their table.

Todd looked at Beverly after the plump woman left with their order and whispered to her, more mouthing the words than making the sounds, "What are Grits?" he asked.

"It's a kind of corn."

After they finished their meal, Todd asked for directions on how to go across country to the highway going south rather than go back the way they had come. The instructions had been long, slow, and complicated.

When they returned to their motor home in the parking lot, he attempted to write them down, but he felt he had forgotten some of them already. Still, he wasn't worried he figured they would find their way.

WINTER

Winter had come with a sudden rage. The only benefit was the fact that it didn't seem that cold around the lodge. The warmth of the sea water, only a matter of yards from the lodge, helped to keep the cold at bay. It snowed two feet the first day, three days later they had five feet of snow around them. The drifts near the bottom of the northern cliff face, were closer to nine or ten feet deep.

The different work groups were working hard just to maintain pathways to everything in the area that needed attention. It was apparent they might need to assemble some sort of structure for a tunnel to the cabin where Frank and Jessie were living if the snow got any deeper. Although the two of them were maintaining a radio watch, at odd and unusual hours, they still needed to be able to get out of their cabin and to the lodge.

A new work group was formed, and they had to work their way down to the boat docks on a daily basis. On the dock they checked each boat over closely to be sure none of them were sitting extremely deep in the water, or that perhaps they had developed a leak somewhere. The crew also cleaned the ice and snow off each boat to keep them from being over loaded with the additional weight.

On occasion, when the group thought it safe, they would take a few of the small boats up to the falls just for the dramatic view. The area around Chatter Box Falls was becoming a spectacular sight to behold. Icicles around the falls were becoming extremely long, some were breaking because of their own sheer weight and lack of a solid anchoring position on other ice. On the east side of the falls a solid sheet of ice was forming from the top of the falls to the bottom. Nearby trees were being encased in ice from the mist emanating from the waterfall as it floated heavily through the air. At the bottom of the falls, where the fresh water ended the first part of its trip toward the sea, an ice field was forming and fanning far out on top of the surface of the brackish salt water. Each time they were up here, they would chop ice away from the Provincial dock so they would have a place to get ashore if needed.

At the lodge, to pass the time of day, many hours were spent learning the skills of others, everyone willing to share their knowledge. Classes were being held in many fields, from wood carving to celestial navigation. One of the popular ongoing lessons was Lyn's teaching anyone who showed an interest how to make home made bread, cinnamon rolls and other baked delights. Each time the baking group had a batch of dough mixed they would put it in bread pans covered with a light cloth material, even the pans for the cinnamon rolls were filled, then the pans were placed on the mantel over the fireplace until the bread dough could rise.

When the time was right they would bake everything in the kitchen ovens. This usually took an entire day. No one concerned themselves with the baking pans taking up a great deal of space around the fireplace on baking days because they all shared in the results. They understood the dough needed the warmth from the fireplace to make it rise and the fire was maintained by anyone nearby.

Although there were always others around, strawberry blond Aireanna, was always nearby when the baked goodies came out of the ovens. She had taken it upon herself to be the one who removed the loaves of bread, the cinnamon rolls, or cookies from their baking pans, then putting it all on cooling racks until it was used for meals. She had developed a knack for slicing bread and it had become her job so each time they needed more sliced bread for an upcoming meal.

Old Hank had taken up the habit of eating his meals in the kitchen, as it was usually warmer than the rest of the building. He preferred the company of the children because they didn't ask him personal questions. Aireanna found out that Hank had been a veterinarian, now retired, and that his wife had passed away several years back. He explained to her that he didn't have any family left to speak of. Hank took a liking to Aireanna because she would see to it that his coffee cup stayed full when he was in the kitchen, and she was partial to giving him fresh baked cookies. He reminded her of her grandfather.

During the day, when there weren't any pressing chores to be done, time was generally passed by playing any one of the many games that had been found in one of the lodge's office closets.

There were many large, and small, jigsaw puzzles to play and some people even resorted to playing them upside down after they had used them right side up. Children and adults played Monopoly, often with the game causing some grumbling as fortunes were made, or lost. Some played Texas hold'em, a poker game, Canasta made a comeback and pinochle was very popular. Some played Bridge and there was always an ongoing chess game, with an occasional tournament of one sort or the other going on.

At the peak of winter they had seven feet of snow as an average depth, and the fresh water was left running constantly to keep the lines from freezing. As it was a gravity fed system, the abundance of water was not a problem. Bathing became a very welcome event that took place during the hours the generator was running so that the bathers would have hot water to enjoy.

Often there would be three of four people waiting their turns for a shower. Anyone, who seemed to be showering longer than the others thought necessary, received polite harassment from those still waiting in line. Those who had taken a cold shower swore it would never happen again.

.

SNOW

The snow had begun much earlier than previous winters in the upper middle states. In the first week alone, Eastern Montana and Wyoming had eight feet of snow, across the north east corner of Colorado and northern Missouri there was seven feet of snow. North and South Dakota, Nebraska, Minnesota, Michigan, Illinois, Indiana, Ohio, Pennsylvania, New York and Massachusetts were all covered in nine to eleven feet of snow. It continued to snow as if there was no end to it. Most of Northern Europe, Russia, and China were all suffering with more snow than in recent recorded history.

Most people throughout the world believed the early snows were taking place because of the amount of smoke and volcanic ash that was in the upper atmosphere in the northern latitudes. Most people were not prepared for a winter of this magnitude either, and many suffered because of it.

At Malibu Lodge, the entire group was planning a celebration dinner for the most productive wood cutting crew. Bob had kept a running inventory on the amount of wood each crew was producing for the winter months. He had started this running inventory in the beginning to keep records of the wood production. He had done this so he would know when they had cut enough wood for the winter. Now this information was the factor in deciding whom the champion wood cutters were. It was a very close race but the results were almost in, and only Bob was aware of the winning team.

LOST AND FOUND

They'd gotten lost going across country. Road signs now seemed to be things of the past. Most were covered in snow so deep they couldn't be seen. Finally, Todd had just given up and turned off onto a gravel road heading toward a house in the distance where Beverly told him she had seen smoke coming from the chimney. In nearing the house Todd had tried to pull off to one side of the driveway just to bet out of the way. It had looked smooth, but wasn't. The motor home slipped into a ditch listing at an uncomfortable angle. Beverly gasped, she felt as though they were going to fall over.

"Damn," Todd had said in disgust.

They climbed out of the motor home through the driver's side door, surveyed the situation, and knew it wasn't going to be easy to get the motor home out. They pulled their coats up tighter around them and started walking toward the house.

As they walked onto the small covered porch, a hand carved sign on the wall provided the name, Kendall, the front door of the small home opened. A man in his late sixties greeted them with, "Well son, looks like yer in the ditch purty deep." Todd blushed and said, "Yeah, I was only lost before. Now I'm lost, and stuck to boot."

Margaret, the woman of the house, walked to the doorway, looked at them and said, "Land sakes, Moe, let them folks in here where it's warm."

Once they were inside, she directed them to the kitchen where she poured Todd a cup of coffee and put water on for tea for Beverly.

Todd explained to Moe what the two of them were attempting to do by going cross country, and Moe had explained to him where they had gone wrong on the turns they had made, then said, "It's gonna be a bit of a chore gettin yer rig out'ta the ditch. No sense tryin it today; it's too late now anyways. We can take a look at it tomorra."

Todd, perplexed, said, "We've gotta sleep in it though."

"Oh no, son. You can't do that, it could tip over during the night. You folks'll stay in our guest house out back. . . .Course you'n I ought'ta go out there an start a fire in the stove to take the chill off it.

With that said, Moe placed his hands on the kitchen tabletop, pushed himself up out of his chair, and walked over to the back door. When he'd pulled on a warm winter jacket, he looked over his shoulder and said, "Comin?"

After they had started a fire in the small wood heating stove, topped off the wood box near the stove from the woodpile outside the back door, the two of them returned to the main house. As they were stomping the snow off their shoes, Todd happened to look at a thermometer hanging on the out side of the kitchen door. It was broken where the red fluid had frozen and burst the bubble at the bottom. Later they were to hear on the news that the wind chill factor was seventy-two degrees below zero in any kind of breeze. Back inside the house, Margaret asked if they were hungry, and Beverly explained that they had just eaten. They visited for a couple of hours. Todd and Beverly explaining that the two of them had left their home in Canada, and had started to explain where they were headed when Todd began to yawn loudly.

"I s'pose you folks'll want'a hit the sack now? Young lady you know how to prime a hand pump?"

Beverly shook her head no, but Todd said, "Yeah. I'll show her."

As the snow crunched under their feet heading out to the cabin, Beverly asked, "Why would we have to know how to prime some pump?"

"Cause they built this place with the idea of getting by without the advantages of modern things like electricity. You know, to survive living here if and when things were really bad."

"Oh, neat," she said, thinking of rustic living, and not sure she wanted the experience.

By the time morning arrived, there wasn't any question they would be here awhile. The motor home was still upright, so to speak, but the side of the motor home away from the driveway was now supporting a huge snowdrift that had blown up against it during the night.

Once they were inside the main house with Moe and Margaret, Todd was apologizing for their forced stay with them. Moe grinned, not caring, but said, "Oh, you'll earn your keep son."

Before the winter was out Todd and Beverly would learn many winter survival tricks. Tricks new to them, but not to older folks who depended on their personal ability to survive.

DOCTOR HANK

Elizabeth came running into the lodge, fear, and tears in her eyes, "Help! help!"

Tony Barton and Jim Harrison were standing near the fireplace. They looked at Elizabeth standing just inside the doorway, and said, "What's the matter Elizabeth?"

As Tommy an I were cleaning the snow off the boats, an while we were getting off one of the boats, Tommy fell off the boat! He's down there laying on the dock hurt an I couldn't help him get up!"

The two men grabbed some nearby coats, pulled them on, and headed out the door saying as they went, "You stay here and get some more help sent down to the dock, okay?"

"Okay." she said, the tears beginning to run down her cheeks again.

When Tony and Jim got down to the dock, they found Tommy shivering from the cold, wincing in pain. "How you doin', Tommy?" Jim asked as he kneeled down near him.

"My leg hurts bad."

"Which one?" Tony asked.

Tommy pointed to his left leg. "This one."

Tony was pretty sure it was broken. "Lay still a little longer, Tom," Tony said as he moved toward a nearby boat. He climbed up on the boat and got the boat pole off it. Then he went to another boat and got one from

139

that boat as well. Once he was back with Tom and Jim, he said, "I need your coat, Jim," as he started pulling off his own.

Then he and Jim pushed the two boat hooks through the coat sleeves and zipped up the fronts, forming a stretcher. They placed it next to Tom's right side and gently moved him onto it. Just as they finished, three others from the group came down the dock. Tony had them pick the stretcher up and carry Tommy back to the lodge. It was slow going on the icy walk. When they reached the land end of the dock, the path up to the lodge was better until they got to the lodge steps. Then it was touch and go again, trying to maintain their balance and not drop Tommy.

By the time they got into the lodge almost everyone was there waiting. They laid Tommy on a large folding table, leaving him on the coats. Quickly they just pulled the boat hooks out of the coat sleeves. Everyone was concerned because they now realized how vulnerable they were without a doctor among them.

Jim, Tony, Larry and Loyd were conferring about what could be done. "We have an emergency doctor's book on the boat," Loyd said. "That should tell us what we need to do."

Aireanna, standing close by, said, "We could ask Hank if he could help Tommy."

Tony looked at her and asked, "Why would Hank be able to help?"

"He told me once he was a doctor of some kind. Veterinarian I think."

"Veterinarian?" Jim grinned.

Then they all looked at one another and Tony said, "Why not?"

Loyd knocked at Hank's door, waited a few seconds, then knocked again. Finally he opened the door, poked his head in and said, "Hank, you awake?" A few more seconds passed. Again, but louder he said, "Hank, you awake?"

"Why, hell yes, I'm awake. How can a man get any sleep with you raising such a ruckus?'
"Hank, we need your help out here."

"Why in the world would you be needing my help?"

"Hank, we've got a youngster with a busted leg an we need you to have a look."

Hank sat up on the edge of his bed, looked at Loyd, and said, "I'm not a medical doctor."

"Please, Hank! You're the closest thing we got to a doctor."

"Doggone it, disturbing a man's rest. If it wasn't for it being a child, I'd stay right here in this warm bed." He climbed up off the bed, all his clothes still on. He pulled his boots on and followed Loyd out the door rubbing the sleep from his eyes as they went down the hallway toward the main room of the lodge.

Once they were standing by the table with young Tommy on it, Hank began to poke and prod Tom's leg, asking him things about how it was feeling and how he

141

was feeling. Finally he said to the men standing near him, "Take his pants off. But do it slow an easy like, you hear?"

"Take his pants off?" Jim said.

"Well, now young fella, don't you suppose it's a bit better to save the boys pants rather than cutting them off?"

Jim, feeling foolish, said, "Yessir." Then he helped Larry undo Tom's pants and slowly remove them, Tommy crying out in pain as they moved his leg.

"One'a you fella's find us something to use as a splint." Three men moved in separate directions at the same time.

Finally, Charles Jensen came back with a couple of wooden slats he'd been able to pull off a wooden packing case he'd found in a food storage room. "This do the trick?" he asked, showing them to Hank.

Hank looked up, took the boards and said, "Yes, those should do fine."

Hank moved up to Tommy's head, put his gnarled old hand on the side of Tom's head and said, "This is gon'na hurt some, but I'll be as easy as I can. You understand, son?"

"I'll try not to cry, Sir."

"You cry all you want, son. There's nothing wrong with a man that cries. Matter of fact he's probably a better man than most."

"Really?"

"You betch your britches young fella."

Hank had Tony and Jim stand by Tom's head, holding his hands in theirs so he could squeeze them when the pain started. He had Loyd hold Tom's right leg firm in his grip so Tom wouldn't thrash it around. Then he had Larry stand by in case he needed a hand with Tom's broken leg.

Hank got into position at the bottom of Tom's feet, took a firm grip on Tom's left leg at the foot and ankle. Then when he got the feel of it he pulled and twisted slightly feeling the bone set in place. Tom screamed.

When they were done, with the splint fastened in place, Tom began to settle down. His body, quivering from the second shock to the broken bone, began relaxing. Hank moved back up to where he could speak with Tom. Leaning over, he said quietly, "You did better than most men young fella, you did just fine."

Tom smiled through his tears.

THE WEDDING

Late in the morning, Larry, Theresa, Ken, Helen, Lyn and Loyd were sitting at a table near the fireplace trying to coax more warmth from the fire, when Jim and Julie, hand in hand, approached them. When they walked up to the group, Loyd said, "Hi folks. Pull up a chair and join us." Jim and Julie did as they were asked, both smiling, waiting to spring their surprise on the others.

"What's up?" Ken asked. He could almost feel the air of happiness about them.

Jim was a little nervous and blushed when he asked, "Is there a minister of some kind in our group?"

The rest of the group looked at one another, searching their memories for a few seconds and Loyd said, "Not that I'm aware of. Do you need one?"

"We want to get married," Julie said, enthusiastically. Her smile spread across her face.

"That's great!" Lyn said. Immediately small tears began to form in the corners of her eyes. She wiped them away with her fingers. Her hand reached out to touch Julie's arm in affection. "Why don't we get the group together this evening and see what can be done?"

That evening when everyone was present for dinner, Jim and Julie announced that they wanted to get married. This was met with great applause. After it quieted down, Loyd stood up and said, "The problem is, we don't actually have a minister."

144

After a few seconds, from the other side of the room, Mary Jensen rose from her chair. Idon't believe that'll actually be necessary. Do you?"

Loyd didn't hesitate. "Not as far as I'm concerned, Mary."

She looked around the room and added, "Is this a problem for anyone else?"

All through the room in rapid succession, no's were heard from all.

Bob Franklin stood. "With this many people to witness their wedding vows, it sure ought to be legal enough. I'm sure God would approve."

Mary and Bob sat down, then Ken stood. "I assume from your comments that the group feels we can progress with this wedding then?" An over all positive response was voiced, the group had decided.

Lyn looked at Julie, then said, "Will this be satisfactory to the two of you?"

Julie beamed, "Oh, yes."
During the next few days, someone with artistic ability, made them a marriage certificate. The printing on it had been done in a Calligraphy style and everyone signed it. It was covered front and back with good wishes and signatures. They planned on giving it to Jim and Julie after the wedding took place.

The women of the lodge had gotten together, and using a portable sewing machine from one of the sailboats, they fitted Julie with a wedding dress. The dress had been made from some of the finest white and light blue spinnaker sail material they had available. It wasn't like anything you could buy anywhere, but it was beautiful.

Jim was fitted out with a dark gray suit that the women tailored to his needs. It had come from Bill Spencer. Bill had kept it on board his boat for the occasional nights when he and Charlene would go out on the town in some of those out of the way settlements that they traveled to. Aireanna spent hours making ribbons for the dresses of the ladies from the same blue spinnaker material.

Lyn, told Loyd, about something she wanted him to make for her. It took him two days to put it together. When he was done, he had a very clean five gallon soap container with a lid on top. The lid had a small piece of threaded rod sticking out of the top with two nuts locked together inside the lid and two outside. A socket, from a wrench set that fit the nuts was fastened to a handle that had been fashioned for turning the rod. All of this fit inside of a plastic twenty-five gallon container that Loyd had cut down. Loyd and Lyn knew what it was to be used for, but no one else did.

Larry had been chosen as the minister. His appointment came about because his uncle had been a minister of a church a few years before his death, and most people felt Larry was more familiar with the intricacies of the church. Loyd was asked to be best man and Ken was to give Julie away.

Lyn, Helen and Theresa were to be Julie's bridesmaids and would attend to Julie's wedding needs and, of course, would be at the altar during the ceremony.

As the wedding day unfolded, enjoyment of the occasion was the source of constant tears of happiness being shed. The entire lodge group was in good humor. Everyone was like family now and they were all involved in some manner.

In the early part of the day, just before the wedding, Lyn had filled the five gallon container Loyd had made for her with a jar of chocolate syrup, canned cream, some vanilla and a few other goodies. Then Loyd placed the container inside the bottom of the twenty five gallon container that had been cut shorter for this occasion. The whole contraption sat on the large sink drain board.

He had the children go around outside the building breaking off icicles. When they were brought in, he placed them between the two containers. Once he was ready he poured rock salt around in with the ice. Finally, snow was also packed in tightly. Then he had his first volunteer start to crank the handle around. The children were kept busy keeping the ice replenished as it melted. A couple of holes in the bottom of the cut down drum allowed the melt water to drain away into the sink. It was getting very hard to turn just before the wedding started.

It was a shaky start, but Larry soon had himself composed and the ceremony went on without a hitch. When Larry said,

"Do you, Jim Harrison, take Julie Martin to be your wedded wife?" Jim proudly said, "I do."

Tears began to well up again in almost everyone's eyes. When Julie said her vows, followed with, "I do," the sobs became very audible from the group behind them. Many of the men's shirt sleeves were being used to dry tears.

When Larry pronounced, "By the power vested in me by the Malibu Lodge society, I now pronounce you Husband and Wife," cheers erupted from every corner of the room.

The reception line never seemed to end. A casual observer would notice that when someone left the line greeting the newlyweds, they would just go back to the other end of the line and start all over again. They did this until they all ran out of sentimental things to say to the newlyweds.

Young Randal went through the line seven times, he'd had a crush on Julie. The wedding feast was a great meal. The ladies who had been preparing the food all day used some of the very rare food items they had been saving for an occasion such as this.

After everyone had settled down from the wedding dinner and the dishes had been picked up, Lyn had them all file through the kitchen in a line for a treat. Loyd had gone ahead of them and cranked the handle until it was again tough to turn. Then as the folks began to arrive he pulled the lid off, and the paddles came out covered with homemade chocolate ice cream. He spooned it off into a bowl for Hank who had also joined the wedding party and who was sitting quietly at one of the kitchen tables. It was the first ice cream anyone had had in months, and the first home made ice cream that most of them had ever had. They knew Lyn was a magician, and this confirmed it.

Much later that night after the wedding, in the radio shack, Tony announced over the ham radio to the world that Jim and Julie were now Mr. and Mrs. Harrison. Much to his surprise he heard a slurred acknowledgment to his announcement. The brief conversation that followed was filled with static, but a time schedule had been set up for their next transmission. Tony was very excited having finally made a contact. In the morning at breakfast he would tell everyone the good news

BLIZZARD

Frank had kept the fire in the cabin's small fireplace going all night. Usually he would let it die down during the night, but tonight he was up and listening to the ham band for any news of the outside world.

As the night progressed he began to hear a creaking noise in the background somewhere. At first he hadn't paid any attention to it because he was trying to make a few of his pre-scheduled contacts. The noise wasn't happening often, but suddenly he actually heard the noise more prominently, and it impressed him. He got up, moved to the fireplace and after tossing another small piece of wood on the fire, he began to walk around the cabin's interior. He couldn't understand where the noise had actually come from.

After his walk around inspection, he sat back down at the radio console and began to swing the dial through the various frequencies trying to pick up an ongoing transmission from somewhere in the world.

Finally the source of the noise came to him. The creaking noise was coming from the roof. The snow was falling heavily, as it had been most of the day. He realized it was now placing a very heavy load on the cabin's roof. The stress was what was causing the roof to creak as it settled under the load. He got up again and began to check the corners of the roof where it met the walls. The main support posts seemed to be okay, as did the walls. In the end he decided to let Jessie sleep, but still, he was nervous. In the morning he would have some of the fella's shovel the snow off the roof.

The blizzard howled most of the night, the cold radiating off the huge windows of the lodge. At the bottom of the windows you could actually feel the movement of air as the cold air slid down off the glass. By morning the west side of the lodge had been covered with snow, but the dawn brought sunshine. A crew of men spent most of the morning just shoveling the snow away from the lodge and off the decks surrounding the building.

Then they went down to the cabin where Frank and Jessie lived, and dug it out, and they removed the snow from the roof. After the shoveling crew left, Frank went out to the back of the cabin and climbed up to where the solar panels were mounted. He scraped the snow off the solar panels with his hands so the panels wouldn't suffer any damage. Back inside the cabin, he glanced up at the small electrical ammeter mounted on the side of a cupboard. The meter was showing that the solar panels were now putting almost two amps into the radio's batteries. Frank knew the batteries had been drained to some degree because of his transmitting, and the snow blocked most of the sunlight they had received. Now, he was satisfied that it wouldn't take too many hours before the batteries would be topped up to their float level again.

He never did tell Jessie that he was afraid their roof might have fallen in on them. It had gotten so cold during the night, and the snow was so deep, that a huge herd of deer had moved down into the protection of the woods on the south side of the falls. With what little food supply there was in that area, many of the deer would perish before the distant spring weather started warming it for the new growth could begin.

151

CRUTCH

Lyn hadn't seen Hank around all morning. As a rule he would usually make some kind of appearance during the late morning, but she knew Hank was a night owl. He would stay up most of the night tending the fire in the fireplace, keeping the lodge semi-warm. He would then rise late and have breakfast in the kitchen. But this morning she hadn't seen him. Concerned, she asked some of the other women in the kitchen if anyone had seen Hank yet today.

"I saw him early this morning," Mary Jensen said. "But I haven't seen him since."

"I wonder where he's gone off to?" Lyn commented.

Mary added, "He was going to go up to the dock at the waterfall I think."
When Hank didn't show up for lunch, Lyn found Loyd in the lodge's main room, where he was sitting with Larry. "Honey, I'm concerned about Hank. No one has seen him since early this morning."

Loyd took her hand, pulled her down for a quick kiss, then said, "Any idea of what he was up to?"

"Mary said she thought he was going up to the falls."

Larry said, "If you want'a go up an have a look for him, I'll go with you."

"Yeah, I suppose we should have a look."

Once they were down at the lodge's dock, Loyd pulled the cover off his dinghy, then tilted the outboard motor down into the cold water. After he primed the motor, it started on the second pull. Larry had been busy bailing out what little water there was in the bottom of the boat. When they were ready, each of them cast a dock line loose without speaking. They motored slowly through the cold chop, eastward toward Chatter Box Falls.

As they rounded the point of land that hid the falls from the lodge, they could see a small boat in the only opening in the ice, and at the dock. They tied Loyd's boat near the walkway end of the dock, but did not see any sign of Hank around. They began walking up the icy snow covered ramp, looking as they went. When they reached the Pavilion, there were signs that someone had been there and had started a small fire. The wind blowing down the hill from the falls would make it hard to maintain a fire and would dampen any resemblance of warmth.

"Holy smokes, Loyd, I hope something hasn't happened to that old geezer. "Me too." They had decided to head up towards the public rest rooms, which were really just decent outhouses. Suddenly Loyd pointed up the hill further. "Look."

Larry looked to where Loyd was pointing and saw smoke coming out of the chimney of the Ranger's cabin. They worked their way up to the cabin following the deep holes in the snow where someone had struggled through here earlier. Larry knocked at the door when they arrived, then not receiving an answer he slowly pushed the door open. Inside Hank sat crowding the small stove. Larry said, "Hank, you okay?" Hank hadn't heard him.

Loyd greeted him a little louder. "HELLO, HANK."

153

Hank jumped, turned around and started in on the two of them. "God dammit, why are you always hollering at me. You could scare a man ta death doing that."

"Sorry, Hank," Loyd said, smiling.

Then he continued, "Where the heck have you guys been? A man could freeze or something before you'd come looking for him." Loyd and Larry both grinned, they knew Hank was okay.

"What are you doing up here, Hank?" Loyd asked.

"I needed a particular kind of stick, if it's any your business."

"You ready to go back to the lodge now, then?"

"Why, hell, yes. I'd have been back earlier if I hadn't dropped the damn oar in the water. It got away from me and I couldn't reach it"
"You mean you lost one of your oars from the boat you came up in?"

"Of course that's what I'm saying. Can't row a damn boat around in circles an get anywhere."

Along side of the stove was a limb off of a tree, with a lot of shavings lying on the floor nearby. It was apparent that Hank had been carving on it with a pocket knife. They picked up his tree limb, helped him to his feet and when it was decided the fire could burn itself out okay, they left the cabin.

Once they had Hank settled in the dinghy, they picked up the bow line of the small boat he had used to get to the dock and took it in tow. Ten minutes later they were back at the lodge, and Lyn had Hank in the kitchen fixing him a hot bowl of soup. He was whittling on his stick again while he waited, the small wood chips just falling all around his feet and grumbling to himself, but loud enough so Lyn could hear him, "Doggone city folks sure put up a fuss for no reason." She just grinned.

That night Loyd got up to check on a noise and watched Hank working on his stick in the light of the fire in the fireplace. It was after three in the morning.

The next morning Tommy was to be seen using a nice hand carved crutch that he'd found outside his bedroom door. It had been placed near the doorknob during the night. Of course everyone knew where it came from.

TEXAS

In a small rural town just south of Lions Texas, the electrical power had been off for sometime. It was long enough that most folks had given up on its ever coming back on. Most of those still living in the area were using kerosene lamps and had reverted to getting by the way they had lived in years long past.

Ray was fussing and talking to himself, "Dang old pump." His frustrations grew with each stroke of the old pump handle, and the results for his efforts. As he pumped, he watched and made the decision that perhaps the old pumps packing gland wasn't tight enough and it might be sucking in air. He found a wrench that fit the packing gland nut and snugged it up a little tighter around the pump's plunger shaft.

Using some of the water he had left in his bucket, he primed the pump again. Suddenly, after he had started pumping the handle up and down, the pump caught its prime. Delighted, he caught the water in his bucket, the pump could now supply them with water from the old shallow well.

When he got back to the house, he entered the kitchen through the back door. Though he had scraped the dirt off the bottoms of his boots on the edge of the back porch step, he pulled them off and left them on the floor of the covered porch and just outside the door. In the kitchen he gently set the pail of water on the sink counter, so as not chip one of the tiles. When she saw him set the pail down, Fran said to him,

"Still having trouble with the pump?"

"Nope. Think Ive got it whipped into shape now. All it needed was the packing gland tightened so air wouldn't leak in and let the pump lose its prime. Shouldn't cause us any more trouble."

"Ray, is there anything more we can do about our drinking water?"

"I doubt it, Honey."

"It's getting awful brackish, and not fit to drink anymore, and cooking anything with it is becoming more and more a chore."

He looked at Francis, his wife of many years, sitting at the small worn kitchen table where she was playing solitaire. "When I was down to the store yesterday, I fetched the last couple bottles a water off the shelf. Everybody is out of good drinking water around here. I reckon we could try boiling some," he said. Then added, "Even then I'm not sure that would do the trick."

Francis didn't like the idea of leaving her home, but times were getting to everyone around the area. Nerves were on edge in many households, others were leaving. "I was finally able to get through on the phone so I called Mama while you were in town. Mama said we would be welcome to move up north to Montana and live with them if we want."

Ray had already thought about moving somewhere else, most of their other neighbors had already left the area. Most of them didn't have an old water well like he and Francis. It wasn't worth the money it cost to have a well dug or drilled. He was also aware that quite a few of the major highways were closed because of earthquake damage, but things were not going to get any better. "Maybe we should think about doing that."

That evening, their conversation became serious about moving out and abandoning the ranch. During their conversation Ray got the old road atlas out of the drawer of the desk he used for the ranch's business. He placed the kerosene lamp on the kitchen table where it would shine its meager yellow light down onto the atlas.

The two of them began looking for a route that would lead them through the maze of highway closures they knew about, or bad weather, north to what seemed a safer place. It looked as though they would have to go across New Mexico, through Arizona, then across Nevada, this of course if the snow would permit. Then Idaho, or maybe across into California and up through Oregon, back across to Montana and to her folks place in Harve, near the Canadian border.

HOMESTEAD

The Harve Montana weather was cold, and the town had been getting some snow. The roads were icy, often covered with black ice, but manageable for those who drove like a sane person. Luckily, for some reason the weather's high jet stream had kept most of the hard weather just to the east of the Harve, Montana area.

"Jake, that you?" Carrie said as she heard the squeaky bottom hinge on the back door as it began to close.

"Of course, Ma, who else'd it be?"

"Oh, just wishful thinking I guess."

"Its only been a couple days since you talked with em. They can't fly you know."

"I know, but I'm troubled about how they're going to get here."

"If they're a coming they'll find a way, don't you fret none," he assured her. Over supper they talked about their daughter and her husband. Carrie and Jake knew he was a good man, good to their daughter, honest, dependable and he could work the land.

"Ma, I was down to the old house by the creek earlier. I don't think it'd take much for them younguns to fix it up some."

Even at this late stage of her life, Carrie had fond memories of the old house. It was where she and Jake had raised Franny. She recalled, 'Them was lean years, they was. Before we did good at raisin' some cash crops.'

Carrie and Jake originally homesteaded the old place, and, as time passed, they bought the rest of that same section of land. They also bought other pieces of land from the bank when times were hard on farmers in the area who didn't have anything put away. They felt bad about buying up land that others had failed on, but knew if they didn't buy it when prices were down, they would never be able to buy it when times were better.

Now Carrie and Jake were getting on in years and couldn't work the land like they did in their early years. But they were making enough money to see them through each year and put some in the bank as well. They leased a large amount of the land they didn't use themselves to other farmers in the county for various needs.

Some just used the land to grow hay. The hay would be used in the winter months to get their herds through the bad weather. Some of the folks moved their livestock to the land they leased from Carrie and Jake. This allowed them to let their own pastures rest. As it was now, their piece of farmland was over one mile across and about a mile and a quarter long. This is considered a fair sized piece of land these days, especially in these parts. In the years before, they used to share crop the land, but now, leasing it was easier and that was money in the bank, too.

"It'll be good having the kids home, won't it Ma?" He didn't say it outright, though he had to agree with Carrie, he thought sure the kids would come home.

"I'm thinking it will be, Pa. I'm thinking it will," she said, looking forward to the company of Franny and the humor of Jake.
NEWS

It seemed as though Jessie was having to beg Frank to get some rest lately. He was spending endless hours on the radio monitoring the airwaves. He'd explained to her that he had to get as much information as he could while the bands were open, and while the few other operator's around the world were on the air.

Most of the news Frank was getting, was bad news. Like the information he found out about last night from a Russian ham radio operator in Bratsk who lived just a few kilometers north east of Lake Baikal. He heard him on the air broadcasting in very broken English.

Frank learned that what had once been the deepest lake in the world had now become the longest lake in the world as well, but at a huge cost of human lives. Lake Baikal in Siberian Russia had, because of earthquakes and shifting plates, become twenty six miles longer, and the old depth of fifty three hundred and fifteen feet was now in question. The lake's depth seemed much deeper now.

He learned that there had been severe fires in the desert country of Texas before winter had set in. The land was now bare of any useable vegetation. The fires were caused by the heat generated by the meteorite's close path to the surface of the earth on its entry, and final collision with the earth's surface just inland from the Gulf of Mexico. The massive amount of earth moved by the impact of the meteor had been pushed, as if by a child's toy, into part of the Mexico basin offshore from the coast. The area off the coast had been three thousand and sixty-two feet deep. Because of the earth's movement, it was now much shallower.

Earthquakes and volcanic eruptions had and still were causing massive loss of land masses and human life. It seemed as though most of the west coast of the United States had sunk from thirty to fifty-five or sixty feet below the surface of the ocean.

Part of the good news Frank could pass on was that whatever the devastation's, people were recovering and joining forces to survive. In most areas of the world it had become second nature for the survivors to police themselves. In most places those people who offended the natural and moral laws were dealt with severely. Local or governmental laws no longer held much meaning, but the communities were policing themselves and crime rates had dropped dramatically.

Frank heard some interesting news from a few cruising boaters with ham radio rigs on their boats. They, and others, now living on their boats, were trying to decide on different locations for a rendezvous of the boating community.

On the East Coast no decision had been made yet. On the West Coast, Drakes Bay, just a few miles north of San Francisco California was the favored spot. It was known to be large and offered good protection from most weather except from the east or the southeast. Very few knew that Drakes Bay on the California Coast, was now even larger. The scheduled event date was open as yet, but Frank believed that a few boaters were already en-route to that destination.

TRIP NORTH

Fran packed their old station wagon with everything she felt they might need for their survival while traveling north. She hadn't liked the idea of the pistol Ray had stuffed under the car's front seat, but she could understand his thoughts of self protection for them on this trip, if it came to that.

They locked the house before leaving, as all of their furniture was still inside. Perhaps they could come back for it at a later date. She was able to put a few boxes of her more prized possessions into the car. The old glass bowls that had belonged to her grandmother were wrapped in several sheets of newspaper, and the picture albums she stuffed into small places between other things. Most of their better clothing was pushed into any open place it would fit, she knew she could iron it out smooth again when they got where they were going.

Ray shook his head in awe as he marveled at the amount of things Fran had pushed, stuffed, or poked into every nook and cranny of the interior of the car. He understood her wants and had allowed her to bring as much of her treasures as she could find space for.

Before they pulled out of the worn gravel driveway, Ray spent several minutes just walking around the car checking the tires and muttering something about their being so overloaded. He checked the engine's water and oil, and finally tied two five-gallon containers of water onto the roof rack along with many of their other possessions. Among those things on top of the roof rack was a small tent, cooking utensils and a small chain saw in case they found trees across the roads they traveled.

It was slow going up Highway 77 through Waco. The crawling pace was caused by the influx of others also on the move. This condition continued until they got through Fort Worth, Texas. Frank had to add water to their radiator on more than one occasion, because of a small leak in the engine's water pump.

Most of the time they were being held up by traffic that didn't seem to be going anywhere in general. When they got to Highway 81, they turned north to pick up Highway 82, and here they turned west across to Lubbock, Texas. They made good time in this part of the back country, and Ray only had to add water to the radiator once, although he was concerned about any water loss.

"I hope this water pump doesn't give out in this back country," he had said to Fran on more than one occasion.

At Albuquerque, the pump was losing more water than was acceptable, and Ray knew they would have to replace it sooner than he had wanted. They wanted to take highway 40 heading for Flagstaff Arizona. They didn't make it.

The engine had begun to overheat badly, and not wanting to cook the engine, Ray stopped their old station wagon on the side of the road.

They waited for the engine to cool down some, then he added more water, drove a few more miles only to have to stop and do it all again. Just before dark they made it to a small campground just outside Flagstaff, Arizona. The people who owned the private campground said there was only one space left, and

Ray and Fran took it. It seemed there were still hundreds of people on the road going some place.

"I'll hitch a ride into Flagstaff in the morning to see about a water pump," Ray told Fran. They were very uncomfortable, but they slept in the car that night. They agreed that in the morning Fran would put up their small tent, while Ray was in town.

The morning was chilly, but sunny. Fran struggled with the tent until a young man came over to help her, then it went up smoothly. The tent just needed two sets of hands to put it together. Ray had left early as he had heard a car engine start near them and had quickly gotten out of their station wagon to ask if the driver was going into Flagstaff. When he returned a few minutes later, he said, "Fran, this gent's going into town and I can ride in with him."

"Okay, I'll see you when you get back."

A little concerned he hesitated, then said to her, "You know where the pistol is if you need it."

"Ray, you know I couldn't shoot someone."

"Just pointing it at someone could do the trick, you know?"

"You go on into town, I'll be okay."

He grinned. Confident she would be okay, he turned and left.

On the way into town in a beat up old Volkswagen, Jimmy asked, "Where you folks heading for?"

"Fran's folks have a chunk of land up in Northern Montana they've made it plain we're welcome. Now this dang water pump's given out."

Jimmy thought about that for a few seconds, not used to being rushed. "I'm thinking there's a junk yard just this side a town. You might want'a talk with the old guy there before going on into town."

Frank had no idea of where any automobile wrecking yards might be so he welcomed the information. "I reckon that's a good idea, thanks."

It wasn't long before they arrived at the cluttered wrecking yard alongside the highway. The fence around it had for the most part, fallen down, only a reminder to those who passed this way as to its boundaries. The sign 'HIGHWAY AUTO PARTS' was also showing its age. Jimmy pulled into the parking area, stopped his Volkswagen just outside the door, and said, "I'll wait here for yuh, whilst yuh see if they got what yuh need."

It was only a few minutes before Ray was back. "Jimmy they have a pump for me, an will give it to me if I take it out, so I'll be awhile."

"I'll wait if'n yuh like?"

"Thanks, but I don't want'a hold you up. I'll hitch a ride back."

"Okey, dokey. Good luck to you, an yer missus."

"Thanks Jimmy. Take care, you hear?"

When Ray had inquired about the pump, he asked about its price and was told it was his for the effort it took to get it out of the car it was in. It took Ray better than two hours to get the water pump out of the car. He'd had to borrow the tools from the owner to do the job, and before he left he'd offered again to pay for the pump.

Joseph, an old man, only said. "I wasn't using it any ways, you might's well have it.

"I'm very thankful, Joe."

"You need any tools for getting it in your car ?"

"No, I've pretty well got every thing I need in the car."

By the time Jimmy got back to the campground from his trip into town, Ray had replaced the pump and the engine had been started. The pump seemed to be working fine.

"Works good," he'd said to Jimmy when he parked his Volkswagen and walked over to them.

"So you folks'll be on your way before long then?"
"Yep, we're leaving at first light in the morning."

On their way the next morning, Ray left the old water pump, and a thank you note, on the doorstep of the auto wreckers for Joseph.

PLANS

Jim was with Loyd and Larry. They were the ones assigned to clean snow off the boats at the docks this week. It hadn't snowed heavy now in a few weeks so cleaning the snow, or now mostly slush, off the boats had become less of a chore. The three of them were taking a break, when Jim mentioned that he and Julie were making plans to head east overland when the weather would allow them to travel.

Until now no one had said anything seriously about leaving. Loyd said, "You know, we'll teach you how to sail a boat if you'd like to travel with us?"

"Yeah," Larry chimed in. "All of us power boaters are scheduled for classes in sailing when the weather permits."

"Thanks, but we've talked it over and we don' think we're cut out for the life of open sea vagabonds. We figured we can pick up a car in The Pender Harbour area, and head east. Julie has some cousins down in Montana somewhere, so we're going to head in that direction."

"We'll be sorry to see you folks leave us," Loyd said, and he knew the two of them would be missed as they had become favorites among the lodge group. Curiously Jim asked, "Where are you gonna get sailboats for you and the others?"

"Well, it won't be long now until we can make some foraging trips out to some of the smaller marina basins in the nearby areas, then we'll see what we can find. Actually we're hoping to get lucky," Loyd said.

WARMING

Late in the afternoon Bill and Charlene Spencer were playing pinochle with Frank and Jessie near the fireplace. It was one of those rare times that Frank had actually taken time off and got away from the ham radio watch he was maintaining.

During the end of one hand of play, they heard a ASSSLLLUUUFFFMMPPHH, noise. Startled they looked toward the source of the noise and saw a large bunch of snow sliding off the roof down onto the deck outside. Some small trickles of water followed flowing from the edge of the roof to the fallen snow pile below, drilling holes into the surface.

"What in the world?" said Bill. The four of them got up and walked over to the window and looked out at the pile of snow now covering most of the deck area outside the window.

"Looks like it must be warming up some," remarked Frank. "Or the snow wouldn't have been soft enough or loose enough to slide off the roof like that."

"Does that mean spring is on its way?" asked Charlene hopefully.

"About high time isn't it?" Jessie said in earnest.

They returned to their card game, relieved somewhat knowing that warmer weather must be on its way.

In a sense Frank had become their newspaper, but this evening during dinner he was regretting giving the latest radio report. His source of information had been from a ham operator in Jacksonville Mississippi.

Apparently the snow had crippled so many states in the north that there had been many lives lost. He reported that in most locations the snow was just so deep no one could get out for food, and almost everyone was out of heating oil and firewood. Some people were able to get to churches or community centers, but frustrations were being replaced with anger. Now they were worried about mass flooding.

CONTINENTS

It was in the early part of March when the last of the earthquakes stopped, though there were still some aftershocks being felt in many locations. Major changes had taken place in the coastal areas of the West Coast of Mexico, the United States and part of the Western Canadian coastline and its many islands. The shifting of the West Coast continental plates was the major cause of the changes.

Throughout the world there were many other plate separations and shifting, and some major changes taking place in several inland areas of the world. The tidal waves that had formed because of the vast terrestrial activity had caused devastation in most small island countries, and a large share of coastal communities throughout the world. Despite the ash in the high atmosphere, from the many new active volcanoes, acting as an insulation factor, spring was coming.

SURVIVAL

Moe was enjoying this winter despite its fury. It was if he had two new children living at home. He was busy teaching Todd the skills of ice fishing, the lake being frozen over for the first time in Moe's recollection. It wouldn't be long, Moe knew, that he and Todd would have to do some deer hunting. He also knew he would have to teach him how to do everything there was to be done with the carcass when they got one. Moe was happy that Todd had, in turn, done anything he could to help out around the place while he and Beverly were there.

Beverly, under Margaret's tutelage had been learning how to can meat. So far it was only the fish that the fella's had been catching. Margaret had assured her it was almost the same process for any meat. Beverly couldn't remember when she had enjoyed being in the country more even in the winter, and Margaret had become like a mother to her.

SAILING LESSONS

Spring was approaching fast despite the cold, and finally the decision had been made. It was time to start teaching the power boaters in the group how to sail and classes were being held whenever the weather permitted. The group ventured just outside the Malibu Rapids Inlet, into Queen's Reach, to do their practicing, but, all of the power boaters were learning to sail. This came about for many reasons, the strongest reason was that the availability of fuel for the hungry engines of the power boats was unknown.

Most of them were finding it fun and were enjoying the quiet solitude of sailing. After each day's sail, when the group got together for coffee in the main room of the lodge, they would huddle close to the fireplace to get warm. Comments were heard from them, like, "My gosh, we didn't realize how noisy our engines were until now. The quiet, and ease of being under sail a surprising new concept to them. Yet the main topic was the little tricks they had learned that day.

Larry and Theresa had teamed up with Loyd and Lyn for lessons, then for diversity they would go sailing with Ken and Helen. The first time they sailed with Loyd and Lyn, on a long downwind reach, Loyd had suddenly turned saying to Larry, who was standing near him in the cockpit of 'Itchy Feet',

"Larry, take the helm, while I go below for a minute."

"What do I do?" he asked.

"Just keep her sails full of wind like they are now and stay just about on this course." With that said, he indicated the course by pointing to the compass, then

Loyd moved away from the helm so Larry could take over. After Larry took the helm, Loyd headed below to go to the bathroom.

Larry soon felt the power of the boat under him. It inspired him as he moved the helm gently from side to side to get the feel of the boat. His mind was on far away sunlit islands.

Just as Loyd finished in the bathroom, the boat eased into an upright position. He heard some shouting and he knew the main boom was about to come crashing across from one side of the boat, to the other. He reached the cockpit shortly after the jibe had taken place to find a shaken and apologetic Larry. Lyn was just grinning, Theresa looked a little frightened.

"God, Loyd, I hope I didn't break anything."

"I doubt it. Most sailboats will take an occasional jibe like that. But it's not something you want to get in the habit of doing."

"Scary, isn't it?"

"Can be if you're not expecting that to happen." Surprised at Loyd's calmness, Larry relaxed and became more comfortable at the helm. The boat had settled again, even with the jib being back winded by the mainsail and producing little in helping to pull the hull through the water. He asked, "Why would you expect that to happen?"

"Sometimes you may jibe the boat intentionally, but you do it with a little more control."

175

"You ready to take her back now?"

"No, you keep the helm. But I will tack the jib for you," he said as he started to shift the jib from one side of the boat to the other. Larry watched Loyd as he removed the jib sheet from the captive cleat, threw two loops off the winch, then begin to pull the slack line, or the jib sheet out on the other side. Then he let the jib sheet loose and began pulling it in on the other winch. Once he had it tacked over, he'd had to winch it in tighter to trim it as it had popped open and full of wind again.

After that incident, Loyd took more care in teaching Larry and Theresa the basics of sailing, and they did pretty well. When Larry and Theresa developed their sailing skills enough, they took Loyd, Lyn, Ken and Helen sailing on Ken's boat. They all knew that Larry and Theresa had passed the final test when they did all the sail changes and tacking from one tack to another without any help. They were acting as a team together. After that it was just a matter of getting more experience.

Finally, the evening came when all the power boaters used someone else's sailboat, and went sailing by themselves. They had confidence now, and one evening they had rafted all the boats together on a mill pond surface when the evening wind had died, and had a pot luck dinner together from the lunches they had brought out with them.

From that point on, they were confirmed rag sailors and would frequently go sailing by themselves. Although it was on someone's else's boat, they were welcome to use them as the trust had been earned in caring for the boat they were using.

One evening, after a day of sailing, they were all sitting around the lodge sharing some of the last wine and discussing the day's sail, when the discussion turned to getting their own sailboats. They'd decided to use one of the fastest power boats in the group to go searching in the nearby marinas for any potential sailboats that might be confiscated by the Malibu Rapids Society. Loyd and Ken would go along as surveyors and to dispense any needed advice.

SHOW AND TELL

Lyn knocked on Larry and Theresa's bedroom door. "Theresa, you ready?"

Within seconds the door opened and Theresa said, "Hi Lyn. Come on in, I'm almost ready."

Lyn sat in one of the two high backed stuffed chairs in the room, watching as Theresa pulled on a sweat shirt over her blouse, then she picked up a wind breaker off the end of the bed, checked her hair in a mirror one last time, finally to say, "Okay, let's do it."

As they walked away from the lodge, Lyn was a little tickled at the thought of showing a city girl things in the country. She walked in a direction that headed them slowly toward Queen's Reach. Theresa walked close alongside her. They were just chatting in general.

"Theresa," Lyn said, "to really enjoy nature, you have to see it. Most people never take the time to look and to become aware of nature as it surrounds them."

Then, just before they reached the waters edge, Lyn stopped quickly. Theresa came to an abrupt halt alongside and said, "What is it, Lyn?"

"What are you aware of right now?" she asked, standing still and noticeably aware of something around them.

"Uhhh." Theresa hesitated, trying to take in her surroundings. "Well I can see some wind wave chop out on the water. Oh, and I can hear some of the fella's splitting fire wood on the other side of the lodge."

The chopping sounds were reverberating off the canyon walls. "And of course I can hear the muted noise from the waterfall."

"And you can see snow on all the high places?"

"Oh yes, I can see that."

"And you can see those pinkish little flowers you almost stepped on?"

Theresa quickly stepped back and looked down where her feet had been, then uttered a slight cooing sound, "Ohh, aren't they pretty." Bending to pick one, she put it close to her nose to extract the small delicate odor. Its sweetness was barely evident, but it was there.

After a few moments, Lyn said, "Now listen." They stood for a few seconds. Theresa strained to hear what Lyn was hearing. Then Lyn added, "There did you hear that?"

"No, what?"

"A kind of shrill, but solid chirp, chirp , chirp."

"I'm sorry, Lyn. I didn't hear it."

"Okay, turn around and listen again."

They had barely turned around and started to listen, when, in the distance, it came again.

"Chirp, Chirp, Chirp."

"I heard it, Lyn! I heard it, :she said excitedly. "What is that?"

"I'll show you in a little while. What's important is that you learn to hear all things, not what you want to hear selectively."

Then Lyn started moving again and they moved down to the water's edge. Once there, she pointed down into the water. Theresa looked where she was pointing and said, "My gosh, Lyn, a starfish with seven, eight, no nine tentacles."

"Also, you can see two different kinds of fish," Lyn commented.

"Oh yeah. Neat, huh? What are those things over there?" Theresa said pointing at another area.

"The small ones that look like small volcanoes are barnacles, the purplish ones are mussels." Theresa had seen barnacles before, she just didn't put the word together with being a small marine animal.

As they walked along, Lyn pointed to some small delicate white flowers they had come across saying, "These are Trilliums." Further along and near the hillside, but heading toward the old cabin now being used as the radio shack, they stopped again. Lyn reached out to a small bushy area near a large rock to point out the small new buds of one or two small open pink flowers and said, "Wild roses."

Theresa leaned over and sniffed, "Lyn, they smell wonderful."

"Most old timey roses, and wild roses, smell better than the new hybrids."

"Really?"

"Yes."
"Look over there at all those white shells along the shore line." Lyn was indicating a shelled beach surrounding McDonald Island that they were now near. "Those are oysters."

"We had some of those in our soup recently, didn't we?"

"We did indeed." Lyn paused a few seconds while she looked up. "Theresa, look up there." She was pointing way up the rocky mountainside.

In a lone bedraggled tree, whose top branches had seen much better days, Theresa saw two large birds.

"That's the source of the chirping noise I had you listen to before."

"They're eagles aren't they?"

"Yes, Bald Eagles."

"How do you know they're Bald Eagles?"

"Actually, it's quite easy. There are only two species of eagles in this area, the Bald Eagle and the Golden Eagle. The Bald Eagle starts getting white feathers on their necks and tails as they molt. These start showing up when they're about, oh four or five years old. This continues until their whole head and tail feathers are white. There are other ways to tell as well, but these are the easiest ways to spot them. Then you can tell the Golden Eagle because they have what some people call knickers.

"Knickers?"

"Yes, they have feathers all the way down to their feet. Kinda like pantaloons in a way."

"Is that right?"

"Yep, plus they have shorter necks and tails."

On their return trip back to the lodge, Lyn had pointed out several more kinds of birds and flowers that were appearing with the spring weather. As they were walking, Theresa stopped, and pointing down to the ground she asked, "What are these little round things here?"

Lyn smiled and said, "Deer poop."

THE BARBER SHOP

Loyd was sitting in the makeshift barber's chair while Theresa cut his hair. She had started cutting Larry's hair for him, and he had mentioned it to Ken, and Ken asked her to cut his hair. Before long she was cutting hair for anybody who asked.

It turned out to be a natural talent for her, and a service that was needed, and she enjoyed doing it. In return, she had a jar labeled 'Perks,' which she kept nearby on a shelf. She had taken over a small downstairs bedroom in the lodge, just off the main meeting room.

Ken, in payment for some of his hair cuts, had built a small platform upon which he had fastened an old, comfortable chair. A chair he had taken from the kitchen.

The perk jar was used by those who were getting hair cuts. They could put a note in it with a promise of something they would do for her in return and done strictly on a voluntary basis. Payment for one of Theresa's hair cuts wasn't actually required. Theresa in turn rarely needed anything for herself, so, when asked, she would ask for something to be done for someone else.

As Loyd sat in the chair getting his hair cut, he asked, "How is your perk jar working out?"

"Oh, it works fine. I cut Lyn's hair last week and she said she would take me on an interesting tour."

Iwonder what that will be all about?" he interjected.

183

"It was great."

"You already collected on that one?" he asked.

"Yes, my curiosity got the best of me, so I asked her for it right away."

"And?"

"It was wonderful. She took me on a nature tour. I've never really been keen on or aware of nature before, but I will be from now on. On our walk she showed me more species of flowers and plants than I thought possible in this area and especially this early in the spring. And I knew there were some birds in the area, but Lyn showed me nine or ten different kinds. Then we went over to some tide pools, where she pointed out more small crustaceans and fish than I had expected to see in such a small area. I think it was the best payment for a hair cut I've had."

Loyd groaned quietly, wondering how he could compete with Lyn's nature tour. He knew it would be difficult to come up with a decent hair cut payment, and thinking he may never ask for another hair cut while they were here.

Instead he changed the topic of discussion. "Theresa, you know some of us fella's are getting ready to go to the outside in search of some sailboats for folks like you and Larry?"

"When are you going?" she asked.

"Within the next few days."

"Will it be safe?"

"It should be." However, in his own mind, he didn't really have any idea of how safe it might be.

When Theresa finished cutting his hair, she said, "There you go, Loyd. Almost like a professional."

"Thanks, I appreciate it. See you next time."

When Loyd got up from the chair, he walked over to Theresa's perk jar, picked up a piece of scrap paper and leaned his nearly bald head back as though looking at the ceiling. He was deep in thought. Finally he picked up a pencil and started to write something on the paper, then he shook his head and crumpled that piece of paper, and stuffed it into his pocket. He picked up another piece of her scratch paper, held it a moment, then scribbled something on the paper. He dropped it in her jar and walked out of the room.

Theresa was curious because she had seen him change his mind. She walked over to her jar and fished out Loyd's promise note. She unfolded it and read. It said, "A moonlight sail for you and Larry." She thought, Another good payment.' Then she grinned. Lyn had said Loyd would try to give her something special for his haircut as well.

DAKOTA

The weather had begun to warm up a little more each day, and Moe had been teaching Todd how to hunt deer. Enthusiastically, Todd was learning tricks the older man had been teaching him during the harshness of the winter. Todd had never been exposed to the need to survive, nor did he ever feel the need to learn the skills of survival, until now. Paying attention to what Moe offered him had become a pleasure. Moe possessed a blunt and outspoken way about him. He was an honest man, one who respected life, and other people, that greatly impressed Todd. The older man also possessed a kind of gruffness about him that Todd liked and began to emulate.

It was still early in the morning, the two of them had been walking for what seemed hours through snow nearly waist deep in the open areas. Then Moe took them in a direction that placed them under the cover of some trees. Under the trees there was very little snow, which offered them some protection. They could move around unhampered by the deeper snow just a short distance away. Suddenly, Moe stopped moving, he turned his slowly, his hand came up and he pointed out the small half starved doe just across the meadow from them. He instructed Todd in a quiet voice.

"Steady son. Don't rush, take yer time." Moe wasn't in the habit of poaching, or shooting a doe either. It was, however, a necessity for them to supplement their larder at home. He knew the winter wasn't over yet.

Todd began resting the rifle across the small limb of a nearby tree. He made himself relax, inhaled, then let his breath out slowly. Just as he had expelled the air from his lungs, and there was no need to inhale or to exhale more air, the point where air pressure in his lungs equalized. He held the rifle steady, and with his thumb up on the top of the stock to direct the direction of his trigger finger's pull, just as Moe had instructed him, and he squeezed the shot off. The booming from the shot dissipated quickly in the softness of the remaining snow around them. He looked up, but couldn't see the doe any longer.

"Damn, I must have missed."

"Tarnation, Boy, you hit her clean. She dropped right where she stood."

They forced their way through the snow to where the doe lay. It was apparent she had not suffered. Satisfied about the condition of the doe, Moe looked around their immediate area. He spotted what they needed, a low limb of the proper size close by the edge of the lake.

"Here gimme a hand an' we'll pull'er over to that tree."

Todd grabbed one of the doe's hind legs and Moe picked up the other one. It was hard work dragging the doe through the deep snow. Todd understood you weren't supposed to shoot does, only bucks, but Moe had pointed out the fact that when you're getting damn hungry you better take what you can get.

When they had the deer under the tree limb Moe selected, they began trampling the snow down so they had an area to work in under the limb. Finished with the trampled area, Moe pulled a small piece of line from the back pack he carried, threw it over the limb and tied it to the front legs of the doe. Then he and Todd hoisted the doe up far enough for skinning and cleaning right on the spot.

Moe reached under his jacket, and from a sheath he pulled out a very sharp skinning knife. He handed it to Todd and said, "It's your deer, you clean'er out." Moe felt it necessary for Todd to take charge of the doe and, that it was his responsibility to finish the job. Moe, being from the old school of thought, didn't want to rob Todd of that hunting initiation.

"I don't know how to do that." Todd didn't have the slightest idea how to even start. He'd never killed a deer before, and now the thought of cutting one open was bewildering.

"I'll tell you as you go along." And so it went. Todd followed Moe's every direction, occasionally catching hell for an almost mistake. When he had first started, Moe had told him how to make a small slit in the still warm hide, then with his fingers as guides, how to open the stomach area by cutting slowly and carefully upward to open the cavity, using his fingers as guides for the blade. He had apparently made what Moe had called a stab and that was a no, no.

"By Jesus, Boy, she's already dead! Just go easy with your work. You cut that doe's gut open with that knife an you'll spill the crap inside'er gut all over the inside the carcass. Then you'll have some terrible meat on yer hands."

Todd felt squeamish when he first started as the doe's warm blood flowed over his fingers while he made the cut. Then he began to settle into the chore ahead, and he felt better as his mind concentrated on Moe's instructions. It had taken much longer than it would have had Moe just done the job himself. But Moe knew Todd might need to know how to do this.

When he had finished, Todd asked, "Now what?"

"Leave her here for now. We'll be needin' some way to get her home, an, I don't figure on packin'er. Come on."

Todd carried the rifle in his right hand as he followed Moe back across the remaining frozen edge of the lake to the lean-to alongside the guest house. There, the two of them pulled the aluminum skiff down off the saw horses and set it down in the snow nearby.

Moe rigged a shoulder and chest harness for both of them and they pulled the empty skiff across the frozen lake to where the doe was hanging. Once there, Todd helped Moe lower the doe into the open boat. The two of them slipped back into the harnesses and together they pulled the boat, with the deer inside, back to the guest house.

Moe laid a sheet of three-quarter inch plywood on the saw horses and slowly gave Todd instructions on how to butcher the deer, and butcher it he did. The next few days Margaret spent teaching Beverly how to can meat. Some they cut into small strips that they put into a small metal smoker that Moe had been keeping in a storage room. When they finished the first few strips of smoked meat, Todd and Beverly enjoyed some of the finest venison they ever tasted. A favorite part, were the back strap steaks they had for breakfast.

ORCA

Someone said, and not speaking to anyone person, "Hey come take a look."

Before long everyone in the lodge was watching the air being exhausted from the Orca's blow holes as the whales came up to the water's surface. The pod of whales worked its way up the sound toward the lodge, some of them moving from one side of the fjord to the other, this was to keep all edible living things in the water racing ahead, seemingly away from danger.

Leading the way in front of the hungry killer whales, harbor seals were trying to escape their captors by swimming ahead or around them, to get away. As it were, the seals were in too loose a group for the whales to attack successfully. With precision the seals were herded through the entrance into Malibu Rapids and the confines of the small fjord which ended at the waterfall.

As they watched, someone asked, "What're they doing?"

Someone else said grimly, "I think they're about to have dinner.'

Finally, most of the pod of whales positioned themselves around the entrance to Malibu Rapids, while three other Orca whales charged ahead into and through the rapids. Inside, these three went to the far end near the waterfall. Once there they turned and started the hunt. The seals began to panic and rushed headlong toward the entrance and away from the present danger. The whales inside were already feasting on seals, while pushing the other seals ahead of them. Outside the rapids, the remaining whales were catching those seals in a desperate search for safety.

Inside the lodge most of those watching were aghast at the bloody feeding frenzy going on nearby. Some turned their backs to the terror going on outside and returned to their previous pursuits. Life's realities outside remained vivid in their minds.

THE SEARCH

Although there were five men in Bob Franklin's small power boat, it rested in the water with plenty of freeboard showing and allowed them a good safety margin. Bob and Betty, a young couple, owned the smallest power boat in the group, it was also the fastest boat. As a precaution the men had a small aluminum boat in tow, with a large outboard engine fastened on its stern. The outboard motor had been tilted up to reduce drag through the water as they traveled.

The plan was simple. They would use Bob's boat to get to the areas where they were going in search of the needed sailboats. Once arriving at their destination, they would use the small aluminum skiff so two or three men could go into the marina to have a look around, and see if it was safe.

The group decided not to go to Vancouver Island unless it was absolutely necessary. This decision was made because of what Jim and Julie Harrison had told them about the state of constant chaos on the island, when they had been there, also because of the distance involved. They had six five-gallon gas cans of spare fuel with them, plus one of the small generators in case they needed to supply electrical power to a fuel dock somewhere in their travels.

They left the dock at Malibu Lodge at first light in the cold early morning hours. The main reason for leaving early was to take advantage of the quiet waters of the fjords they had to pass through before the afternoon winds came up. The weather had been nice in the last few days, and, because of this, they expected the weather conditions to remain about the same.

Today's destination was an area to the south, known as Secret Cove, it contained several small marinas and was on the mainland. They all agreed that if there were any boats left in the area, this would be the place.

The trip to Pender Harbour was smooth, and they made it in just over four hours. Though they had stopped only long enough to fill the fuel tank of Bill's boat, 'Hot Shot', and to have a quick bite to eat, they found every vehicle in the parking lot had one flat tire.

They were in a hurry, and were all a little restless. Not much was said about the flat tires, but everyone figured it must be accidental. Within an hour they were outside Pender Harbour heading south. As they approached the light on Francis Point, of Francis Peninsula, Bob asked, "Loyd, what course direction I'm supposed to follow?"

"Uhh, ooh. . . lets see." He pulled a folded chart out of a plastic storage bag and looking at it briefly, said. "Steer a course of 123 or 124 degrees. When we get near our destination, we should see a light on the south end of 'Turn Again Island'. We pass it to our port, and Secret Cove should be straight ahead."

"How long will it take to get there?" Larry asked."

"It's only about seven miles, so it won't take very long at all."

They had to go a little slower because the long ocean swells had started, and they were thankful there wasn't much wind chop on the water. Loyd, watching the rocky coast line said, "Fellas, I thought I saw the light, at least part of it. This should be the entrance we're looking for." His fingers pointed inland where, what had been a high breakwater, was nearly underwater.

Arriving just outside the Secret Cove area, Ken and Larry, as planned, climbed into the small aluminum boat, easily started the outboard motor and cast off leaving the others in 'Hot Shot.' Just before they left, Loyd said, "It's a large basin in there. We'll motor inside slowly and wait just inside the harbor entrance for you guys. You might check out the marina to the north first, then the ones to the east after that."

"Okay, will do," Larry said.

"We'll see you fella's after bit," Ken said cheerfully. He gave them a wave goodbye and with that they were moving away rapidly. Loyd, Bob, and Bill Spencer waited nervously. They continued watching the direction the small boat had gone, the swells raising them up to a height where they could see all the way into the Secret Cove area. Then they would be at the bottom of the swell's trough where they couldn't see anything.

They waited a few minutes, put the boat's engine in gear and motored slowly toward the entrance of Secret Cove. Passing the entrance light, located on their right, only the top of the light itself occasionally raised slightly above water. The rocks it was built on were well below water now. They entered the harbor basin and turned left to get out of the incoming swells and into the lee of what land remained.

Finally Bill said, "I think I see them coming back." They started looking in the direction he had pointed and could see the small boat heading their direction. Ken stood up to wave at them as they approached.

Bob cranked Hot Shot up to full power and it was only minutes before they were alongside the boat with Ken and Larry aboard. The wake caused by the two boats went rushing off toward the far shoreline. After Ken and Larry were back aboard Hot Shot, and had the aluminum skiff tied to the stern, they explained that the situation, as they saw it, it looked promising.

Larry and Ken both confirmed, "We didn't see a soul around anywhere, but we did find a problem."

The rest of them looked at him, Bill said. "What?"

"At a dock in the East end, I came across Wave Runner.

Loyd said, "Neil and Sandi's boat?"
"Yes, but there's bad news about the boat."

"And that is?"

"There's dried blood all over it."

'Oh my God! Do you think he killed her?"

"Nope. I think she killed him. Or, at least tried to. It looked like he was bleeding badly and tried to get away. The cockpit had blood all over it, then there was a trail of blood going across the dock to the other side. I think he was trying to get away, and fell off the edge of the dock. Probably drowned."

195

By now all of them had looked around the area, as if they might be next. Loyd said. "Why do you think she killed him?"

"Not that I really wanted to, but I went on board. I didn't find a body, but I did find all of his stuff."

"So?"

"So, her stuff was all gone."

"You think she's still around?"

"I couldn't even guess."

They sat mulling this new piece of information over for a few seconds, then Ken said, "Well, we better be getting on about our business, don't you think?"

Each man was a little apprehensive, but they had to finish what they had started. Larry continued with, "Most of the boats are in the marina at the north end. We looked there first. There are a few in the other two areas, but mostly the areas to the east are full of power boats.

They motored slowly northeast to the northern marina, tied up to the fuel dock and began looking around. They stopped at each boat and looked each of them over as they went along. After they had looked at them all, Larry, Bob and Bill decided which ones they liked best. One was a classic wooden hull that hadn't received the care it needed.

Loyd popped his head up out of the deep bilge area of the classic hull saying, "She's fulla dry rot. Too bad cause she would have been a good sea boat."

"Gosh, I kinda liked her," Larry said. "She's got nice lines."

"She would have," Ken said. "She's a William Garden design."

When Loyd found dry rot at the water line, they decided to leave it in search of another vessel. Once they decided which boat each man wanted, they took each boat in turn to the fuel dock and topped its tanks off. While they were at the fuel dock Loyd stayed behind while Ken took the other three men on a shopping tour for sailboat supplies. They had to look in all three of the prominent mooring areas, but they found spare anchors, various kinds of line, and ended up with forty six gallons of bottom paint they could share with the others.

Very little food had been found. It seemed the area had been stripped clean, and they only saw one vehicle. When they were ready, Loyd and Ken stayed in Bill's powerboat, Hot Shot. They would take it back up the coast and into Malibu Rapids themselves. Plus, this way if one of the new sail boaters got into trouble, the two of them could merely motor over to the boat that had a problem to offer advice or help.

As they left Secret Cove, Loyd looked south. He could see that Welcome Passage was now much wider, and could tell that Smuggler Cove, which was once a small hidden bay nestled back behind large rocky ledges and boulders, would now be a large open bay.

Possibly, even non-existent.

Had anyone taken one last glance back into Secret Cove, they would have seen a wisp of smoke coming from a chimney on the side of a hill near the eastern most marina, a pair of binoculars trained on their departure.

The agreement was that they would not sail the boats today. Instead, they were just using the engines to find out if there were any problems with them. They were to meet back at Pender Harbour where they would again fill all the fuel tanks and check the town over for more goods to take back to Malibu Lodge.

Loyd had given them a course of 303 or 304 degrees to follow for the return trip. It was a slow trip going back because each of the new sailboat owners was checking all the engine gauges often to be sure everything was working properly. It was late afternoon when they finally tied to the fuel dock at the yacht club in Garden Bay.

They filled the fuel tanks of the three sailboats and Bill's boat, Hot Shot. Then they made a trip into the center of town with the pickup that had been used by their group before loaded it with three loads of canned foods to transport back to the lodge. The store shelves were now almost completely bare. The storage areas in the back were equally barren. They spent the night at the yacht club with an early morning start time scheduled.

Once again they were only going to motor. They would wait to learn to sail these boats after they were back at the lodge. The morning trip started smoothly and the boats, all in a row, looked impressive. If you didn't know better, you would have thought the area was populated. The trip went well. An afternoon breeze came up and without saying anything, the last boat in the group soon had a jib up and was running down wind. As that boat passed the one in front of it, that boat in turn hoisted a jib. Then as the two boats passed the next boat in line, it too had a jib up, until they all were motor sailing with jibs set. Loyd and Ken just smiled at each other when this event started.

The friendly mini race showed signs of confidence among the new sailors, and the enjoyment of playing with their new boats. Arriving at the entrance into Malibu Rapids, the sails were quickly dropped to the foredeck and the boats motored easily in through the quiet entrance. At the dock, they were greeted by the entire lodge group shouting and waving. Everyone was happy and jubilant at the sight of the boats and the return of the sailors. It took better than an hour for the whole group to tour the three new boats. The enthusiasm brought forth a promise from the new owners for an open boat event on the upcoming weekend.

BOAT SHOW

The additional boats the fella's had found, and brought to the Malibu Lodge Society created an idea that just seemed to grow on everyone. Before the weekend arrived they all agreed that they would have the first, and the last, Malibu Lodge Boat Show. Even the weather was cooperating with their plans. The morning started out cloudy, but the sun began to peak through in the late morning, warming the air slightly.

By lunch time everyone was moving about the dock from boat to boat. Many conversations about boats, or some boat related subjects, were taking place on the main dock. Many of these conversations were taking place between folks who had just finished visiting one boat and before they moved on to look at another boat. Sometimes you could find the owners of a boat you were visiting on board and sometimes you didn't.

On every boat's main salon dining table or a convenient chart table, a note pad and a pen or pencil were to be found. This allowed anyone who had questions about how some particular piece of equipment worked could leave their name and question on the note pad. They did this knowing they would be given an answer later.

To a casual observer, it was apparent that these people were no longer just acquaintances, but more like close family now. By the end of the following week, several boat owners were involved in making or helping others make modifications to their boats. Many were small modifications, but all were designed to enhance the owner's ease of doing something, or to make life aboard more comfortable.

PREPARATIONS

The week following the boat show, found the group meeting each evening, discussing the new sailor's progress and self confidence, answering questions for them and offering advice. For no apparent reason, the discussions started turning to the time when they would be leaving the area, and where they would go from here. One Saturday they decided a group meeting should be scheduled for the purpose of making these decisions.

The following Wednesday at seven O'clock, the entire group was seated around the main room with a low fire still flickering in the fireplace. The evening weather was one of the warmest they'd had in sometime, and occasionally even doors were being left open during the daytime to let the fresh air circulate through the building. Everyone was enjoying the difference in the warming weather.

There was a lot of idle chatter this evening and there didn't seem to be any type of order to the group. It looked as though no one was going to take charge and start things, so Loyd stood up and rapped a spoon against his empty teacup. Its clink, clink, clink caught everyone's attention.

The reality was most folks at the lodge had just accepted the fact that Loyd would run the meeting as he usually did. Loyd hadn't planned on these things being his responsibility, they just became his as if inherited. He didn't mind chairing and directing the meetings, but most often, he ended up passing the speaker's position over to others in the group who had something to report.

With everyone's attention he said, "Gentlemen, and ladies of the Malibu Lodge Society, I think we should start this meeting." Loyd paused a few moments, took a deep breath and continued, "It almost saddens me to start this meeting, because in my heart I know it's the beginning of the end of this wonderful group, and the good times we've had here together."

During the few quiet moments that followed his mentioning this fact, he could see by the expressions on their faces that they all felt pretty much the same way. It hadn't really dawned on any of them, until this moment, that, yes, this was the beginning of the end of this part of their lives. None of them were sure they wanted it to end, because they had enjoyed the time together so much.

Even old Hank wasn't so sure he wanted them to leave, and he was someone who valued his private time, and the solitude here at the lodge in the winter months. This had become his home even before this group of people had come to stay, but he had enjoyed this group more than the others. This group had been more like family to each other, not stuffy or out of touch with reality.

Loyd continued, "I'm sure most of you are aware Jim and Julie, our newly weds, are going to go inland when they leave us. They're going in search of some of Julie's cousins who they believe may be living in Northern Montana."

With some hesitation Julie stood up, and with tears visibly running down her cheeks she blubbered out, "I, . . .Oh god, I, . . ." She stopped, blew her nose and tried to resume what she wanted to say, "I don't want to leave any . . ." She couldn't continue, and unashamed stood sobbing quietly.

Jim rose to stand beside his wife. He was also, noticeably emotional. He swallowed quickly, then said, "Julie and I have grown to think of most of you as our family. But we do feel a need to go in search of our other family. Though you will always be in the neighborhood of our hearts."

Julie could only nod her head in agreement, her hand holding a handkerchief to her nose. Then Jim guided her back down into her chair.

By now several people were crying openly, and it took several minutes for the group to compose themselves enough for Loyd to continue the meeting. A small stray tear was running down his own cheek.

Loyd said, "I'm sure all of you have heard about Wave Runner so we'll not go into that. He looked quickly around to see if any hands had raised. Does anyone have anything they want to say to get this meeting started?"

Ken raised his hand, stood and said, "For those of you who might be interested, Loyd, Larry, myself, and our wives are considering heading down the coast. Possibly to rendezvous with the flotilla in Drakes Bay on the coast of California.

It seems to be the main meeting place on the west coast for boaters who're interested in selecting some place to live together and with interests in starting a new community."

Charles Jensen stood and asked, "Where is this new community going to be?"

Ken replied, "Chuck, I haven't any idea actually. But Frank has heard ham radio reports from boaters on the move, about several places, and that's what this group of people are getting together for. They're wanting to pool all the information from everyone they can, and then decide which way is the best way to go."

"Will they be wanting feed back about this area as well?" Came a voice from someone else in the group, someone who didn't stand to be recognized.

"Yes, they will," Loyd interrupted. "The Northwest could be a very important area for their consideration."

By the end of the evening, most of them knew that they would go along with the main body of the group. Some were undecided as their offshore experience was either nil or very limited. Loyd then asked if they would all submit their thoughts and ideas, about when the departure date should be and it was left at that.

The next morning as Loyd and Larry were checking dock lines on the boats at the lodge dock, Jim Harrison approached them.

"Morning, Larry, Loyd," Jim said as he nodded his head to them.

"Good morning, Jim," both answered as they looked up.

"What's up?" Larry asked.

"Julie and I figure we're ready to start our trip east whenever you fella's can take us out to Pender Harbour," he replied.

Loyd stuck his hand out and Jim took it. 'We'll be sorry to see you two go, but life goes on."

Larry asked, "When did you say you wanted to go?'

"I'd guess as soon as we can."

"How about day after tomorrow?" Larry said.

"Works for me," Jim replied. Then he added, "Thanks fella's. See you later." Then Jim turned and walked slowly back toward the lodge.

"Why did you want to wait until the day after tomorrow? We could have gone tomorrow,"' Loyd asked.

"Because we need to have a going away party, don't we?"

"Oh my god yes. We'd better go tell the ladies."

OVERLAND

The party they held the night before, had been a huge success. Several gifts were given to Jim and Julie, plus names and addresses of friends who could help, should they need them. That is if these contacts were still available. Someone asked Ken, "Do the kids have any money?" and he didn't have any idea. So the two of them started making the rounds of the lodge. As it turned out, a considerable sum of money had been put into several envelopes to be given to Jim and Julie before they left. One contained Canadian currency, the other American. No one had any idea if either currency had any value presently, but they had given freely.

Now on the dock in the half light of dawn, with the engine warmed up on the tug boat, the crowd waved goodbye as the tug moved out away from the dock. Lyn and Theresa were at the controls while Loyd and Larry coiled dock lines and put them away. Jim and Julie were wiping tears from their eyes and putting their belongings inside the main wheel house of the tugboat. The trip out to Garden Bay was a quiet one. Just idle chatter flowed among the six of them, as if nothing of importance was about to happen.

After they arrived at Pender Harbour, they put the spare tire on the pickup truck they had been using, then Loyd, Larry and Jim went in search of a suitable automobile for their trip south. They'd been going door to door looking at every vehicle they came across. Then, in one garage they found a Land Rover in very good condition, with a note on the dash that said, "Keys in the kitchen, if you need it, use it."

Surprised, but understanding, they went through the unlocked back door of the house where they found the car keys hanging on a small nail on the side of a kitchen cupboard nearest the back door. A note was on the ceramic counter top near the sink, it explained how this family had taken their small motor home and were headed for Tennessee. When Jim turned the key in the ignition, the jeep started instantly and purred like a kitten. He was just as surprised to see the gas tank was full.

As Jim backed the Land Rover out of the garage, he came face to face with two old men staring at him through the driver's side window. "What do you think you're doing with this car, eh?"

Loyd and Larry, who had been inside waiting for Jim to back out, were surprised but were quickly outside in case they were needed. "Who are you folks?" Larry asked.

"We live here, and who are you? Eh."

They felt like thieves, but Jim said. "My wife and I are heading south, and the folks who own this car gave us permission to use it, if we need it, and we need it."

The tension eased, and the conversation took a turn that indicated there were other older people around town who had decided to stay. Loyd offered. "We'll be back through here in the near future on our way south. When you folks see us, come on down and we'll have a crew of people do whatever we can for you folks before we leave."

Smiles came over the faces of the older men, "Young man, we'll be looking for you."

When the three men got back to the yacht club, they carefully loaded Jim and Julie's things into the back of the Land Rover. Then, knowing it was time, everyone began embracing. Hugs and kisses were given and some moist eyes were apparent as Jim backed the jeep around in the driveway. Suddenly he stopped.

Julie jumped out of the jeep and ran back to the four of them. She threw her arms around Lyn and Theresa. "Bye, Moms," she said. Then she ran back to the waiting jeep. As the four of them watched the jeep disappear into the distance, a slight audible sigh was heard from the four remaining. Then they all turned and started toward the tugboat. Loyd and Lyn walked hand in hand. It had been like watching their own children leave home. Before they left the lodge Loyd had offered Jim one of the group's small electrical generators, but Jim had declined knowing they could find one on their trip if they needed one.

They arrived back at Malibu Lodge just before dark. The lodge group was very quiet that night.

ENCOUNTER

Jim and Julie stopped at a small bed and breakfast in Langdale their first night on the road. They'd asked the owner about the ferry schedule and were told that the ferry was operating, but the fares were reported to be much higher now. The reason was, it was no longer a government function but was now a private enterprise. The cost of their room was reasonable but only because there weren't many people traveling through this part of the country now.

The next morning when they boarded the ferry, they paid one hundred and eleven Canadian dollars for their fare on the ferry. They told the ferry operator that that was all the money they had. They had more but they kept it locked away in a secret location on the jeep. Julie was irate over the price, but she knew this was the only way to get to Vancouver and the main highways.

Later, when the ferry had landed at the terminal on the far shore, they were again on their way. When they passed Hope Canada, she and Jim began to relax a little. Even then, they knew they had to be on their guard against thieves, or worse. Just in case they might need it, they had picked up a small generator on the outskirts of Vancouver and some camping equipment as well.

They were able to make very good time on the highways as there was little traffic on the roads. The second night they spent in Coleman Alberta Canada. While they were in Coleman, Jim had to pay a very high price for fuel, but they didn't have a choice, they needed the fuel. The next afternoon they crossed the border at Coutts Alberta, finally stopping for the night in Shelby, Montana.

During this part of their trip they encountered a little snow on the ground here and there. Enough to suggest there had been a great deal more snow in the very recent past. Even yet you could see the different layers of snow. You could see thin lines of ash or soot between the layers of snow.

The morning sun was shining, but Ray's sense of humor was under a dark cloud as he looked under the hood of the old station wagon. Fran was looking on helplessly. As she did so, out of the corner of her eye, she saw a young couple coming down the stairs of the motel where she and Ray had stayed the night before. Their car had been acting up again and they had needed a good night's rest and showers. Ray hadn't slept well, but Fran knew he felt better today about things in general.

As they walked down the stairs, Jim saw the man looking under his hood and stopped near him saying, "Problems?"

Ray looked up and smiled, "Yep, dern oil pumps just about had the course."

"Where're you headed?" Jim asked.

"Over ta Harve. A hunert an thirty, to a hunert an forty miles east," Ray replied.

"She gonna make it?" Jim asked understanding the concern.

"I doubt it." Ray said frankly.

They all stood there looking under the hood when Julie said, "Can we pull them with the jeep, Jim?"

"Oh, we wouldn't want to trouble you folks none," Fran replied, not meaning it.

"I'm sorry," Jim said. "My name is Jim Harrison and this is my wife Julie."

Ray stuck his hand out and said, "I'm Ray Carlson and this is my wife Francis."

Then, "Ray, why don't we go have a look at our jeep and see if we can tow your car?"

Ray shook his head, both men understanding what it would entail to undertake such an endeavor. He muttered an "Okay" then they walked over to the Land Rover to have a look. Ray knelt down, and looked under the jeep. He said, "Looks strong enough if you're really interested in towing us. It's a long haul though."

"Well, what the heck, lets try it," Jim replied. "Apparently we both have the time."

While Fran and Julie had gotten inside the station wagon and chatted, Ray and Jim searched the area within a few block's radius and finally found some chain and a section of two inch pipe, plus some strong nuts and bolts. With these parts, Ray and Jim worked up a tow arrangement that would keep the station wagon from running into the back of the jeep by running the tow chain completely through the pipe. Then the pipe was placed between the front of the station wagon to the underside of the rear of the jeep. Satisfied, they tried it out for a couple of blocks, then they started their trip east together.

Jim, Julie and Fran were in the jeep. This allowed Fran to give them instructions on where they were going while they traveled. Ray stayed in the station wagon to steer it during the trip. While they stopped for lunch, the two men checked out their towing system. It seemed to be holding up well, even the nuts and bolts holding the ends of the chain loops closed were still good and tight.

With the arrival of late afternoon they were nearing the outskirts to Harve Montana. There had been some harrowing moments at first, because Jim had never towed anything in his whole life. He caught on quickly with instructions from Ray, then things went smoothly.

HOME

They had been driving along quietly for the last hour or more, with only occasional spurts of chatter as Fran would point out some familiar landmark to them, when suddenly Fran exclaimed, "Goodness me, I'm sorry. We have to turn right on this next road."

Jim quickly reached over and rolled down his driver's side window, put his hand out and down to indicate to Ray that he was going to slow down. Ray was expecting it and began pushing on the brake pedal in the station wagon to slow both vehicles. When Ray saw Jim's arm go out and up he knew Jim was preparing to turn right. This was confirmed by the right turn signal flashing.

As they turned onto the old gravel driveway, Jim looked up as they passed under an overhead sign saying MARSDEN and he said, "Where should I go when we get up to the house?"
"Probably out toward the barn," Fran said, unsure herself. "You'll see it.'

As the two cars neared the house, Carrie, who had been setting the table for the evening meal, looked up and said, "Jake there's a couple a cars coming up the drive."

Jake, who had been ready to nod off, got up from his rocking chair, walked to the front door and opened it. He looked out at the drive. "Carrie, love, I'm thinking you might want'a come take a look at this."

Carrie ambled slowly over to the door, wiping her hands on her apron out of habit. She looked at the two vehicles coming slowly up the drive. The front one had a hand out of the passenger side window and was waving. The second vehicle, a station wagon, had a hand out the driver's window, waving.

"Lordy, lordy. Pa, I'm thinking that that's the kids coming home." With that, she pushed open the sagging screen door, rushed across the old painted porch, her hands holding onto the wide rail at the edge of the steps, to steady herself as she went down the steps. Then she headed out toward the barn where the cars had stopped. Jake was close behind her, the screen door left slightly ajar.

Fran was out of the jeep as soon as it stopped. She ran around the back of the station wagon and into her mother's arms, both of them shedding tears and hugging.

At the same time, Jake was throwing his arms around Ray, the male code of behavior long forgotten and saying, "By grab, Son, we're powerful glad you're home."
"By golly, Jake, we're mighty glad to finally be here ourselves."

"Who're your friends here?" Carrie asked as she stopped for a quick look around but pleased to have them whoever they were.

"Oh, Mama, these are our friends, Jim and Julie Harrison." She continued saying, "Jim and Julie this is my dad, Jake, and my mother, Carrie." The men shook hands and the women gave quick hugs.

After a few moments of greetings, Carrie said, "My goodness, we best be getting back to the house. I've got bread in the oven, and we can set some more places for dinner." She then took hold of Fran and Julie's hands and began leading them back toward the house.

Jim, feeling somewhat uneasy said, "Gosh, folks, we weren't expecting to stay for dinner."

Jake smiled and said, "Ain't no sense of your arguing with her, Son. She's made up her mind. . . you folks are staying."

Jim said," What about the cars, Ray? They okay right there for the time?"

"Yep. We'll leave em right there and have a look at em in the morning," Ray remarked. He knew only too well that Jake and Carrie would insist that Jim and Julie stay at least overnight, if not longer. That's just the way they were.

Jim thought to himself, "Tomorrow?"

OUTWARD BOUND

When the final day of departure arrived, the lodge was left with everything having been cleaned and put away, as if it had been prepared for its first group of visitors in this coming season.

Everyone had been preparing for days, washing clothes and bedding, topping up fresh water tanks, and food storage areas were crammed with everything every boat could hold. Slowly, and with some reluctance, on the last morning the group had started their boat engines letting them warm up. They were severing a tie with a place that had been home to them through what could have been a very hard winter. It was hard, but because of the unique strength of their personal ties with one another, it had seemed easier.

The final hour had arrived, and they knew they needed to leave. If they caught the ebb tide they could use it to help pull them out of the Fjords on the start of their new journey. Hank was standing on the side deck of the lodge watching the events unfold. Some of them had already cast loose from the dock and were circling out away from the dock, waiting until everyone had cast off and was ready to go. The tugboat was left tied to the dock with instructions taped to its control panel on how to get it started. They had taken great pains to show Hank how to get it running. The instructions were left there in case someone came along and needed to use it, and if Hank wasn't able to remember what he'd been told as to how to get it running.

There were three power boats left at the dock as well. It had been explained to Hank that they may not have enough fuel to go out to Pender Harbour more than once, whereas the tug had a full fuel tank and was very dependable and very seaworthy. The keys for the power boats were left in the ignition switches.

Larry and Loyd were the first two boats that motored out through Malibu Rapids, the others followed close behind. Hank stood waving goodby to each boat as it passed by the south end of the lodge and out through the rapids. Everyone waved back in return and shouted their goodbyes. Some were worried about Hank being left behind, but they knew it was his choice.

They all agreed that they would sail if conditions were favorable for the new sailors to gain some experience before putting out to sea. The first stop planned was to be Garden Bay to top up the fuel tanks of all the boats. From that point on, it would be spontaneous decisions as to where to stop and when. The VHF radios were all tuned to channel sixteen, the emergency channel, to listen for one another and any other radio traffic they might chance upon.

SUPPER

Over dinner the conversation was mostly about how the four of them had come to be at Shelby Montana simultaneously. How, with the help from Jim and Julie, Ray and Fran had been able to get home. Finally, during a lull in the conversation, Jake, speaking to Jim and Julie asked, "Well, now, what've you young'uns got planned next?"

Jim spoke up saying, "We think Julie's got some relatives around this part of the state somewhere. We thought we might try to find them."

Without hesitation, "Why don't you folks stay here with us until you kin find'em?" Carrie asked.

"Oh, we wouldn't want to impose ourselves on you folks," Jim said.

"Oh, don't you fret none, Son," Jake said, then continued, "You'd be doing us a favor if you was around."

"How's that?" Jim asked curiously.

Jake didn't hesitate at all. "I've got a number of things to be done around here, and quite a few of them are a bit much for me. They're chores needing some young fella's ability."

"You mean we could help out around the farm?" Julie asked sounding a little excited.

"Sure enough could, sure enough," said Carrie as she rose from the table, her hands busy as she began gathering dinner dishes, then she headed for the kitchen. Fran and Julie got up and started to help Carrie clear the table.

The men were still talking about Jim and Julie staying on at the farm as Julie came back into the dining room. Jim said, "It's okay by me. Julie, what do you think about staying here while we look for your family?"

She hadn't heard the whole conversation, but had already made up her mind that if Jim was comfortable here, she would be. It was as good a place as any to start their search. "Sounds great to me, as long as we can help out around the farm."

Later in the evening Jim and Julie were shown a room upstairs that would be their room while they were here. They slept very soundly that night under the heavy quilts and clean sheets. This is a comfort often only found on old farms.

They slept well, that is, until five thirty in the morning when a knock came at their door. "Breakfast in five minutes folks," Jake said when he knew they were awake. He grinned as he turned and walked back down the hall, then down the stairs toward the kitchen.

Carrie saw him coming and said, "Well, Pa, you thinking they'll do okay here on the farm?"

"If they make it to breakfast this morning, Ma, they'll be here every morning," he commented.

It didn't take five minutes before Jim and Julie were sitting at the kitchen table having coffee. They were somewhat disheveled. Their eyes were still adjusting to the light. Their hair hadn't been combed, and Jim needed a shave, his shirt hadn't been tucked in, but they were there.

Jake smiled, turned and winked at Carrie, and she smiled back. She knew the two of them would enjoy having these kids around.

Ray and Fran joined them a few minutes later, saying, "Morning folks."

HANK

Hank woke up early as he usually did, his bedroom chilly. He dressed quickly in the cold not bothering to shave and headed for the warmth of the kitchen. It was dark and empty. . . then he remembered the reason why. "Doggone it. Coffee isn't made either."

Already he missed the group of people he'd kinda gotten used to having around. Remembering he'd only been up once last night to put more wood on the fire, he went into the main room of the lodge, and forced the remaining coals of the last fire in the fireplace back to life. Once he had it going, he put a small sauce pan of water on the fire grate with some coffee grounds in it. "Doggone it. Terrible thing for a man having to fix himself camp coffee in the morning."

Sometime during the day when he had the generator running he'd make a big pot of coffee and put most of it in the large thermos bottles the group had left behind. "Bless em," he said to himself. "Bless'em, everyone," he said as his gaze fixed on the wooden crutch he'd carved for Tommy. It was leaning up in a corner at one end of the fireplace.

In the beginning, as the group readied to leave, he'd considered going out with them. Then he'd decided, 'Naw, too complicated.'

Hank missed the folks more as the days went by. At the same time, he was glad to have the lodge back to himself, the peace and quiet settling to him. He also knew he might be alone at the lodge for sometime to come. The group had left him a hunting rifle and ammunition, and he knew how to use them, plus a large supply of food. He could fish and use the smokehouse as he needed, and Lyn had left him a good selection of seeds for a vegetable garden. The tugboat and the power boats were there but he doubted if he would ever use any of them. He felt like he had the world at his finger tips. He was pleased. It didn't take him long to fall back into a comfortable self-sustaining routine.

PENDER HARBOUR

When the group arrived in Garden Bay in Pender Harbour, they all rafted together in the center of the bay. From here each boat would take its dinghy ashore when needed. As it turned out, the next morning nearly every dinghy was tied up to the remnants of the yacht club dock. Every boater had turned out to help fetch and carry for the older folks who had remained behind.

Loyd and Larry were delegating chores to the Malibu Lodge Society members who were volunteering, they were in the company of George Renault. George was a very active man in the community, and had taken on the responsibility to see that as many needs of his flock would be taken care of as possible.

Frank and Jessie were instructing two other couples on how to use the ham radios that were still in the home where theirs had come from.

Several men were cutting firewood, and the children were stacking it before it would be covered with large tarpaulins. The people in town had used a good portion of the lumber from the local lumber yard for fire wood this last winter. Three people had died during the winter because of the cold, and because there was no electrical power available in the area.

Ken and Bill rigged up a generator at the back of a small community hall. Then they explained to three of the men how to start, and maintain it for their use. Its primary function was supply power to heat the hall when the group got together here for meetings.

After it had been hooked up, Bill pulled the main breaker fuses out of the fuse breaker box. If he had not done so, the generator would try to power the whole community and not just the community hall.

Several cars and trucks were started, their batteries charged, and another generator attached to the power panel at the gas station. Its main breakers here were also removed. Fortunately, the stations fuel tanks were nearly full. With the amount of driving that would be done around the area, it was doubtful the gas in the tanks would ever run out.

The group from the boats spent three days getting things as ready for those remaining behind, as possible. Everyone was thinking that no one still here would ever leave here.

KEATS ISLAND

After leaving Pender Harbour, the next agreed upon destination was to be Keats Island to the south. The new sailors would try their first solo sail, knowing that they would have help nearby should they get into any trouble. The distance they were going to cover today was about thirty-three miles of open water. They expected it to be an easy trip.

Loyd and Lyn, sailing their boat 'Itchy Feet' in company with Ken and Helen on 'Time Out,' had agreed to sail at the back of the group, while Charles and Mary Jensen would sail at the front. Charles and Mary had also planned to lead the group into the anchorage at Keats Island. Shortly after they left Pender Harbour, they had fair winds out of the northwest and sails went up on every boat. The fair winds gave them an easy beam reach all the way down the coast line. Loyd and Lyn were able, at one point, to catch up with Larry and Theresa on the sailboat they had renamed 'Senseless Two.' They were waving and smiling, obviously having a good time.

What had been at one time a shallow passage into the area of Keats Island and Gibson was now much deeper and required no concern. As Loyd and Lyn were entering, Loyd said, "The depth sounder says we have thirty-nine feet of water here."

"Didn't we find about a fathom or so here last time we came though here?"

"Yeah, and it's low tide according to the tide tables."

"So this area has sunk over twenty-five feet, or better."

"Seems like it."

By five O'clock that afternoon, Lyn was at the helm while Loyd was lowering their anchor down into the muddy bottom. They, having arrived last, had to anchor because the first boats in had taken the mooring buoys that were placed by the Canadian Government in these waters as a park service.

There were some remnants of the government docks still in place, but the broken planks could be a hazard, especially at high tide. The buoys apparently had enough chain to allow them to still reach the water's surface, with the exception of high tides.

It was only a short time before everyone was on the beach with a fire going to fight off the evening chill. The remaining part of the island seemed to be deserted despite the many homes that surrounded its shore line.

The stories of the sail down the coast were being traded and a feeling of accomplishment was prominent in the minds of the new sailors. This short trip had brought forth a renewed confidence in the new sailors leaving them ready for the next segment of their journey. Everyone would be surprised a the changes they found in the coastlines, nothing was as it had been.

THE OLD PLACE

Jake and Carrie had stayed around long enough to show Ray and Fran some of the changes they had made at the old place where Francis had been born and raised. After Jake had finished showing his son in-law the small workshop that had been added, they walked under the car port that was also a new addition but was really just a pole barn in disguise. In the kitchen once again Jake said, "I stuck some new boards in this here floor, afore we put the new linoleum down." He was pointing down to an area of the kitchen floor in front of the kitchen sink.

"Looks good too," Ray commented. He could see a slightly depressed area of the floor where the new boards had been a little thinner than the original planks that had been used to build the building so many years ago. He figured he'd have to take the linoleum up so that he could put some sort of spacer under it to build it up to the original floor height. Other wise, if any water was spilled, or leaked out onto the floor in that area, it would just cause a puddle. If he found this be a necessity, he would just do it quietly. There wasn't any sense in disturbing Jake over it.

As the two men entered the small living room, they found Jim and Julie talking with Fran and her mother.

"Pa, did you forget, I got to get my chores done?"

"No, I ain't forgot." He started toward the door. "You folks can do without us, so we'll be gitten back to the house now."

Then Fran's folks left the four of them alone. They needed to go back up to the big house as there were other farm chores that needed their attention. After the folks were gone, Jim and Julie stayed behind to help with whatever needed to be done. Ray and Fran didn't have many things to move into the old house, most of their belongings were still in Texas. Jim and Julie were going to stay at the main ranch house with Jake and Carrie because it was larger and had more room.

Ray said, "Well, let's get started."

It took the four of them all morning just to clean the old place. Though the old house had been kept up and maintained, it still needed some extensive deep cleaning. Late in the afternoon while Julie and Fran started putting things away in the kitchen, Fran said, "You fella's can go do what you like. We're just gonna finish up here, then we'll be done for the day"

"Okay honey. We can start moving some of the extra furniture from the big house down tomorrow if you like," Ray said, as he and Jim were leaving. The old attic in the big house had a wide assortment of furniture stored there. Some had been left by friends or relatives who had planned on coming back for it, but never did.
That afternoon as Ray and Jim were at the barn, they pushed the station wagon inside to keep it out of the weather while Ray was making repairs. Ray had started removing the oil pump from the station wagon so it could be fixed or replaced if needed.

"How's it going Ray?" Jim asked, as he looked down into the engine compartment, while leaning over the fender. He'd been wandering around the barn looking at its old style of construction and was surprised at the simple methods used to build it, yet it seemed so solid and stable. Now he had returned to where Ray was working.

"Good. Find me a nine sixteenth's box end wrench will you?"

Jim turned and began to rummage through a tool box on a small wooden crate just behind him. Finding the wrench he said, "Here you are," he handed the wrench down to Ray's waiting oil covered fingers.

"Thanks," he replied, as he began to remove the last bolt.

While he was standing there, just killing time, Jim had explained how he had come by the jeep. "So it's not like I own the jeep." He was silent a few moments then he added, "The reason I told you about the jeep is because I want you folks to feel free to use it if you like."

"Thanks, we will if we need to." Then he added, "As a rule Jim, on the ranch here, it's pretty well understood that anything here can be used by anyone, any time."

"Oh." Jim was kind of surprised at the assumption that anything here could be used by anyone at anytime. "Lessen you say other wise, that is."

"Oh, no, that's fine with me." Jim was rather beginning to enjoy the informality. It's like family, he thought.

The next day they moved more furniture from the attic down to the old house than they thought it would hold.

Just about the time they finished, Jake came down to pick them all up. Jim and Julie, along with Ray and Fran were given a tour of the whole place, and a look at all the out buildings. When they'd finished the tour Jake said, "I've made up a list of things needing done. You fella's sort it out as to who gets what chores."

"I'll give Jim all the hard stuff, 'cause he's younger," Ray said to Jake with a smile on his face. Jake nodded his approval.

Jim was pretty sure that wasn't how it would be, but by the time the second week ended, he wasn't so sure after all. He hadn't worked this hard in his whole life. A basic schedule was set up for what needed repairs and what chores needed to be done, and when. Life on the farm had begun. Later Julie could be heard singing, and Jim was whistling while he worked. It was apparent they were enjoying being here, with a family and a place they could call home.

NEAH BAY

The group was appalled at what they were seeing in their travels. It appeared as though most of the coastal area had sunk at least twenty to thirty feet deeper into the water. Beaches and land spits that had been some protection for many homes, and shore side facilities were gone. Most of the shoreline homes had disappeared entirely.

Even the breakwater at Neah Bay was submerged. It now served only as a surge control to keep the basin quiet at low tides, but at high-tide it allowed for a constant rolling sensation from the entering seas. The base of the lighthouse nearby was still above water but just barely. It could only be reached safely at low-tide. Time would see to its demise. The light was no longer tended by the Coast Guard, and the automatic lighting system had failed. Any marine traffic was left to fend for themselves.

The Makah Indian tribe who owned this land were fighting to maintain some kind of control over their lands here and to repair the breakwater as best they could. It would take time but it could be done. Supplies were hard to find and expensive, but as the group of boats arrived, they were taken care of. It was the first group of boats to have traveled through this area in months. Loyd asked one of the local fishermen about the conditions down the coast at La Push, one of the few small ports along the Washington coast.

He had replied, "La Push is gone."

"Gone?" Loyd said in a questioning voice.

"Gone," he replied, then continued, 'Most of it disappeared with the earthquakes, then the high wave came. When it came it took most of the rest of La Push with it. Now the sea washes way into the basin on every high tide. Of course the high rock is still there but it won't provide much in the way of a protection from the seas."

STORM

The first day and night at sea after the group had left Neah Bay were pleasant, sunny, and warm with some cloud cover and fairly quiet dark blue seas. All of the boats were being steered by wind vanes or electric auto-pilots, their occupants had only to watch time pass.

As darkness began the second night at sea, Loyd noticed the barometer was coming down and said, 'Lyn we better be sure things are put away. It looks like we may have some foul weather coming up." Then he called the other boats on the VHF radio and expressed his concerns. They agreed to keep in touch by radio and not to bunch up close together. They sailed on between ever darkening clouds with possible rain showers held in check. The winds were light, but everyone could sense the coming changes. Knowing they could do nothing about it, left only the choice of waiting.

As the following dawn approached, the winds began to increase. By early afternoon all the boats were all down to two reef points in the mainsails, this to ease the pressure on the rigs. When the dark of night enveloped them again, all the boats were hove to. The folks on board were keeping the boats as comfortable as they could in the bumpy seas. Loyd and Ken had convinced everyone to keep a heading of 240 degree south by southwest. On this course they were heading for warmer weather on longitude 125 degrees knowing this would keep them clear of any dangers of land.

The wind was blowing spray from wave tops over the boats and they were taking white water over the bows constantly. It was miserable outside in the raw weather where the spray would sting your skin as it traveled horizontally.

Ken passed the news that the wind had reached thirty-eight knots as it howled through his rigging, with gusts of forty plus knots. Seas were running about twelve to fifteen feet as they were normally measured. Loyd chuckled as he thought about this height. This was how waves are measured by the weather bureau but what the sailor at sea would be looking at was very different. The waves he was looking at were twenty-four to thirty feet from top to bottom.

The radio was kept busy during the night as some of the boats were experiencing their first trip offshore and their first storm at sea. Loyd and Ken found themselves talking often, more as a manner of letting the others know that it was okay to be out here. Just a delay in their trip. Larry and Theresa found it comforting as did most of the others, as they listened to Loyd and Ken's idle chatter on the radio.

Loyd was complaining about a small amount of water that was coming in through his anchor chain hawser hole. And Ken was teasing him about having to manually pump the bilge every hour or so.

The next morning Loyd found that the jib sail tied down on his foredeck had come loose. As he watched each boarding wave threaten to tear it to shreds, he knew that he would have to go out onto the foredeck to tie it down again.

After telling Lyn of the sail condition and what had to be done, he called Ken on the radio and advised him of his condition.

Ken asked, "Call me back once you're back inside."

"Will do Ken." Before he could get his foul weather gear on, he heard Bill Spencer call him.

"Loyd, is it really necessary for you to go outside during this storm?"

"I'm afraid so. No sense letting a perfectly good sail go to Davy Jones locker if it can be saved."

"Okay - but be careful."

Loyd put on his safety harness and headed topside and into the raw weather that Mother Nature was seemingly holding them in. In the cockpit of the boat they had a large safety ring installed so that they could snap a safety harness to it. Lyn, who was along side of him, snapped her harness to it as well. She knew she wouldn't have much to do, but it was a safety factor for her to be here in case Loyd needed anything, or if he got into trouble when out on the foredeck.

"Honey," she said, "you be very careful okay?'

His reply was, "You know how it is, one hand for the boat, one hand for me." Loyd inched his way out onto the pitching foredeck, fastening the clip from his safety harness to any item that would keep him from going over the side of the boat with one of the many waves that were washing over her. Finally he reached the foredeck and frantically tied the jib down. Then he retreated aft to the safety of the cockpit. As he watched the wave action from the cockpit, it only took another five minutes before the jib was loose again. Loyd asked Lyn if she would like to take a turn just for the experience.

When her reply came back a sugar coated, "AHHOONNEEYY" and then, "NOT A CHANCE." he went forward again.

This time while he was on the foredeck tying the jib down much more securely, he was buried under a ton of salt water from a boarding wave breaking over the bow. He watched and, sure enough sea water flowed down the anchor chain into the forepeak chain locker. From here he knew it would find its way into the bilge through limber holes. He pulled one of his gloves from a pocket of his foul weather gear jacket and stuffed it into the hole around the anchor chain. "That should take care of the problem," he said only to the storm winds as they lashed him with salt water.

Late afternoon found a wide spread of boats in the eye of the storm. Everyone was beginning to perk up and it made Loyd feel bad to have to tell them that now they had to go through the other side of the storm. Loyd had been through many storms at sea and was thinking of how interesting it was in the eye of a storm.

He found it interesting to observe that the seas are still very high but mostly just peaks jumping up everywhere. There was no pattern to them, just lots of single peaks of water everywhere and it was never comfortable. Spirits were lifted some just to have the meager warmth of sunlight showing through the eye of the storm.

Forty-five hours after it started, the storm passed. The seas were still rolling, but the sun was warmer, and the radio was busy with excited talk and lifted spirits. It took all day for the group to gather again. They found they were just above the Columbia River on the Oregon Coast.

"Well, folks,' Loyd called out on the radio, "what say we nose in toward the coast and see what things look like?"

Several voices cracked the air during the next few minutes. Some of them could care less, but most were curious. A few were ready for a few days rest. Because they had ended up being well over a hundred miles out to sea after the storm, it took them all night to close on the Oregon coast.

COAST LINE

If they hadn't confirmed where they were, with the use of their GPS and celestial navigation, they wouldn't have believed it. The Columbia River bar jetties were non existent. What remained was just a giant opening, mostly awash with breaking surf. It looked as dangerous as it must have looked in the early nineteenth century to the old sailing masters who plied this coastline.

Loyd and Lyn wanted to enter the Columbia River and explore for a few days because they had been here in the past and they wanted to see what had happened. They weren't concerned about the rest of the group, because they all had enough experience by now to look after themselves.

When Loyd contacted the others by radio about his intentions, there was some chatter between many boats. Radio protocol long gone, everyone just joined in the conversation whenever they had something to say.

Larry and Theresa made the decision to join Loyd and Lyn in their exploration, then Ken and Helen altered course to follow them in. Charles Jensen called back to them on the radio and said, 'We wish you well. Perhaps we'll see you down the coast later."

"Thanks Chuck. You folks take care and good sailing to you." Loyd hung up the radio mike and looked out the starboard portal. The other boats were altering their course for a southerly direction. Then he turned toward Lyn, and she saw a look of concern on his face.

"They'll be okay," she said.

"Yeah, probably."

COLUMBIA RIVER

The three boats waited while they watched the wave activity before them and their intended path into potentially quieter waters. The seas washed over what was left of the breakwater that had taken so many years to build. Only the tops of the channel marker lights and the towers at Fort Canby to the north were visible. To the southeast the waters lapped at the cement remnants of Fort Stevens. Sand Island in the past that claimed so many square riggers was under water, waiting for the unwary soul to venture its way once again. Most of Clatsop spit was awash as well.

Finally the river mouth was quiet enough to allow safe passage over the bar at slack high tide. With very little left to determine a better passage through the mouth of the river, all three boats kept a constant vigil and watched their depth sounders as they moved slowly into the river.

Loyd was steering 'Itchy Feet' with an electric steering device he had built from an old auto-pilot that had gone belly up. Its flux gate compass had quit working properly so he'd removed it and changed the unit into something he could use.

With a long cord to the steering device in his hand he stood up on the cockpit seat to get as good a view as possible. This afforded him some comfort in steering the boat in through what was now a fairly quiet surf. In this position he could see a sand bar before he ran aground on it.

Once through the treacherous entrance, they motored upstream more easily but slowly. About eight or nine miles inland from the bar's entrance, he looked south to see a large estuary. This at one time had been the Skipanon River. The river was still there, but now it emptied into the wetlands much further from the original bay than it had been. There had been two marinas in there.

Five hours after they entered the mouth of the river, they anchored between what was left of Lois Island and the old Mott's Basin to the southwest of their anchoring position. Here they would be out of the river current and some of the weather long enough to rest for a couple of days.

The fellas took a dinghy and explored the remnants of what had been a small community on the nearby John Day River. It was too clogged with debris to consider it seriously. They returned to their boats with plans for the next few days exploration.

They intended to explore upstream and to stop at every island that looked like it had any potential for habitation. Three days later they were standing off Puget Island, and after some discussion they decided to push on. Late in the day they anchored in behind Wallace Island, a small cove protecting them from the weather and the river current.

DRAKES BAY

The thick California coastal fog had engulfed Drakes Bay as the last two sailboats were feeling their way in through the white, damp wall. During their conversations by radio with other boats already in Drakes Bay, Charles and Mary Jensen had discovered friends from the past were there. Joanne, Phil and their daughter Christie were on their boat Swiftwater. They were already anchored deep into the bay and talking by radio with Chuck on 'Stars' Trying to help them find their way through the thick fog so they might anchor close by Swiftwater.

Chuck and Mary knew they would have to be very careful in their navigation to come in blind in this heavy fog, as there were rocks lurking in some areas close to shore and an old wharf left over from bygone days of the clipper ship trade and fishing in this area. Their friends from the north were following close behind.

Earlier as they approached from offshore, Mary watched the blank wall of a fog bank as it rolled in from the open sea. Chuck was at the helm and they knew they could not possibly beat the fog bank to the bay. Knowing this, Mary took a compass bearing on the end of the peninsula at Drakes Bay. This would give them a compass course to follow and allow them to clear the end of the peninsula safely. She then called the other boats following them by radio, suggesting they change their course for Drakes Bay entrance immediately.

They agreed, and all boats came about on a port tack and a new course. As they entered Drakes Bay, they could just barely see the rocky point of land through the fog and the group was following close by Stars stern. Joanne, on Swiftwater, relayed a message by radio that they were anchored in five fathoms of water.

The group had all taken their sails down and were under auxiliary power, each moving very slowly through the fog covered bay. Mary was plotting their position on the marine chart for the area. Telling Chuck to turn left or right, while she watched the depth sounder, keeping them on the five fathom curve knowing this would lead them to where Swiftwater was anchored.

Other boats from their group were dropping their anchors as they went along, with each agreeing to all join up later. It seemed to take forever as Mary watched the depth sounder to track their position over the sea bottom. Suddenly Chuck said, "Holy smokes! They're right in front of us."

Chuck motored past Swiftwater a short distance, dropped a stern anchor, then motored back close along side of Swiftwater where Phil and Joanne waited. When they were within range, Mary threw a mooring line to them. It was caught on the first toss. Once they were rafted together, Chuck shut the engine down and the four of them hugged one another across life lines.

Phil said, "When you folks get squared away come on over and we'll fill you in on the events as they stand."

"Will do," replied Chuck, eager to hear the latest news.

COLUMBIA RIVER

The six of them spent two weeks exploring the upper Columbia river basin but had returned to Wallace Island the day before. Now ashore on the island they were all sitting on a large log about one hundred feet from the water's edge on the southwesterly side of the island. Previously they had spread out in several directions to explore the island. Loyd and Lyn had explained how they found an area where there were nineteen large logs laying in clumps. Apparently they were left there from a broken log raft.

"I'd guess they were swept into the clearing by a large wave similar to the one that came down Queen's Reach while we were at the lodge."

Larry asked, "So, you're telling us we'd have plenty of fire wood?"

"No, no, no. We'd build houses on top of them. Then if we had another flood, the houses would just float. We'd be high and dry and safe."

Larry and Theresa told about finding a fresh water spring near the northern end of the island. It was on a slight rise in the ground and could be developed.

Ken and Helen, in their search of the island, had found an area nearby where they could build a dock out into the water, and an area for a garden, plus they had seen several deer on the south end of the island.

They all agreed that the island had some promise as a home site.

HOME

They started work in earnest the next day clearing the area chosen for their homes to be built on log rafts. Before the week was out, they had found a small nearby town that had survived, and where there were some hardy folks enduring a new beginning themselves. Gasoline was expensive but available.

With two of the chain saws they'd kept from the Malibu Lodge, they began cutting the nineteen logs to accommodate the timbers for the foundations needed the floating homes. Over a period of weeks they gathered enough milled lumber from the river to build one home at a time. Often spending nights together under one finished roof until the three original homes were built.

The first year had been a tough one, planting gardens, canning meats and vegetables in preparation for the coming winter. By the end of the year they were well established. They had solar panels in place for charging batteries, which in turn supplied them with A.C. voltage with the help of some D.C. invertors. Also, they were able to create hot water by running it through black plastic pipe on their roof tops.

EPILOG

After Fran's folks passed away, she and Ray moved into the larger house. Jim and Julie, who were still with them, helped work the farm and moved into the old place. The ranch was once again very productive in producing much needed crops to keep most of the families in their area in fresh produce.

Jim was now a foreman over seven hired hands, with Julie looking after their two children. Jim and Julie never did find her relatives though they had driven hundreds of miles around the entire area without a lead as to where they had gone.

Ken and Helen, Larry and Theresa, Loyd and Lyn had taken up residency on an island in the Columbia River, where they built homes atop logs that would float should the river rise higher than expected during winter storms. Here they grew gardens and had chickens that roamed the island, sharing it with wild deer.

They kept three small power boats tied to a small dock on the south side of the island. These were used to retain access to the mainland when the need arose. Some of their older children had joined them and their grandchildren commuted to school on the mainland each day unless the weather was bad. If this was the case they would stay with friends on the mainland until conditions were better. Years later Loyd and Lyn moved into a small home on the Rogue River. They lived to a ripe old age watching sunsets, and many small children in the area came to know Lyn as "Grandma Lyn". She still baked cinnamon rolls and cookies to share.

Frank and Jessie who had gone south with the rest of the original group had moved ashore into a small abandoned home on the Inverness Peninsula North of Drakes Bay, California.

Charles and Mary Jensen took up residence on a small island in the California Delta, while Bill and Charlene Spencer moved up into the Sierra Nevada Mountain Range.

Tony and Maria had just dropped out of sight, but were believed to have ended up living in the California Delta country.

Sandi Crawford ended up spending all of her time helping the older folks who had stayed in the Pender Harbour area. They thought of her as an angel.

Todd and Beverly found her relatives in Tennessee, but spent the next three summers helping Moe and Margaret get ready for the coming winter months.

Hank passed away in his sleep two days before some families from the interior decided to move into Malibu Lodge. Bob and Betty Franklin were lost at sea.??

Other books written by Donald Boone

CHOOSING LOVERS
Why spend years with the wrong lover.
Find the one that best suits your needs
and enjoy freedom from sexual hunger.
ISBN 1-882896-04-1
EAN 978-1-882896-04-2

CYCLES & RHYTHMS of INTRIGUE
Most of life, if not all of it, contains cycles.
From the birth of any event it will find
its natural rhythm and follow it to the
end. Is life fated, read the answer in this
book.
ISBN 1-882896-07-6
EAN 978-1-882896-07-3

THE CHESS COACH
Becoming one is easy, and it can be
very rewarding. If you play the game
and have time on your hands, consider
becoming a chess coach.
ISBN 1-882896-08-4
EAN 978-1882896-08-0

THE SEA PILOT
In this age of sailing vessels, we no longer fear sailing
over the edge of the flat world, and we find our way
with compass and chronometer. This was not so when
this story took place.
ISBN 1-882896-09-2
EAN 978-1-882896-09-7

CHESS STORIES THROUGH THE AGES

This book, 'Chess Stories Through The Ages,' contains stories that have been passed from one generation to the next down through history. From why 'White moves first, and an unknown story of 'Helen of Troy, found in, 'The Sacrificed Trojan Horse.'

ISBN 1-882896-10-6
EAN 978-1882896-10-3

THOSE WHO PLAY CHESS

Knowing how your opponent plays chess, his or her favorite pieces and their quirks, are a definite advantage to you in this game. Especially if you play in tournaments. This book will provide you with information on them as individuals, and that of their personalities. You will also find lists of historical players with the same kinds of individualism's and personalities to help guide you in your defense at the table.

ISBN 1-882896-11-4
EAN 978 -1-882896 -11-0

IMPACT

Meteors have been haunting mankind since the beginning of mankind, and they still do. This story is about one of those celestial bodies that does not miss the earth on its path around our sun. Like meteorites of the past, the damage it causes when it strikes the earths surface, is devastating. However, many survive and this story is about how one group came together to get through the worst of the affects.

ISBN 1-882896-12-2
EAN 978-1-882896-12-7

IFPublications
mgn.editor@gmail.com